"There is a small problem with your credit card,"

the hostess, Angelique, said to Emma.

"A problem?" Emma echoed.

"Yes," Angelique replied. "It was turned down."

"There must be some error," Emma said confidently.

"Certainly," the hostess agreed diplomatically. "Do you have another?"

"Of course," Emma said.

Angelique ran the new credit card through the approval machine. Rejected, read the message.

They tried another. Rejected.

"As you say, there must be some error," the hostess said coolly. "But surely you will settle the matter."

Emma's heart was pounding. *Oh, my God,* she thought. *She actually did it. My mother canceled all my credit cards!*

The SUNSET ISLAND series
by Cherie Bennett

Sunset Island
Sunset Kiss
Sunset Dreams
Sunset Farewell
Sunset Reunion
Sunset Secrets
Sunset Heat
Sunset Promises
Sunset Scandal
Sunset Whispers
Sunset Paradise
Sunset Surf
Sunset Deceptions
Sunset on the Road
Sunset Embrace

Sunset Wishes
Sunset Touch
Sunset Wedding
Sunset Glitter
Sunset Stranger
Sunset Heart
Sunset Revenge
Sunset Sensation
Sunset Magic
Sunset Illusions
Sunset Fire
Sunset Fantasy
Sunset Passion
Sunset Love

The CLUB SUNSET ISLAND series
by Cherie Bennett

Too Many Boys!
Dixie's First Kiss
Tori's Crush

Also created by Cherie Bennett

Sunset After Dark
Sunset After Midnight
Sunset After Hours

Sunset Love

Cherie Bennett

Sunset Island

SPLASH

A BERKLEY / SPLASH BOOK

If you purchased this book without a cover, you should be aware that this book is stolen property. It was reported as "unsold and destroyed" to the publisher, and neither the author nor the publisher has received any payment for this "stripped book."

SUNSET LOVE is an original publication of
The Berkley Publishing Group.
This work has never appeared before in book form.

SUNSET LOVE

A Berkley Book / published by arrangement with
General Licensing Company, Inc.

PRINTING HISTORY
Berkley edition / June 1995

All rights reserved.
Copyright © 1995 by General Licensing Company, Inc.
Cover art copyright © 1995 by General Licensing Company, Inc.
This book may not be reproduced in whole or in part,
by mimeograph or any other means, without permission.
For information address: General Licensing Company, Inc.,
24 West 25th Street, New York, New York 10010.

A GLC BOOK

Splash and *Sunset Island* are trademarks belonging to
General Licensing Company, Inc.

ISBN: 0-425-15025-9

BERKLEY®
Berkley Books are published by
The Berkley Publishing Group,
200 Madison Avenue, New York, New York 10016.
BERKLEY and the "B" design
are trademarks belonging to Berkley Publishing Corporation.

PRINTED IN THE UNITED STATES OF AMERICA

10 9 8 7 6 5 4 3 2 1

For Jeff, who follows his dreams

Sunset Love

ONE

"I'm in heaven," nineteen-year-old Samantha Bridges said with a sigh as she closed her eyes to kiss her boyfriend, Presley Travis.

"I thought you hated camping," her best friend, Carrie Alden, teased her as a thin pillar of smoke rose from their campfire and twisted into the night Maine sky. "I thought you said you were allergic to fresh air and marshmallows."

"Right," her other best friend, Emma Cresswell, joshed good-naturedly. "Didn't you tell me that the only time you'd sleep on the ground would be when you were six feet *under* it?"

All six of the girls and guys sitting around the crackling campfire—Sam and Pres, Carrie and her boyfriend, Billy Sampson, and Emma and her boyfriend, Kurt Ackerman—cracked up. Carrie and Billy were sitting side by side, while Emma and Kurt were stretched out on their stomachs, their legs intertwined. It was past midnight, but none of them wanted the evening to come to an end.

"See, this just shows I'm having a positive effect on you," Sam retorted. "You're developing a sense of humor. The old Emma was humor-free."

"That's probably true," Emma allowed. She looked lovingly at Kurt, whom she had almost lost forever. "But that's because I wasn't very happy then."

But I'm happy now, she thought, her eyes shining. *I'm so happy that I never want this moment to end.*

Sam leaned her head against Pres's shoulder. "Do you believe in fate?"

"Whoa," Pres said in his melodious east Tennessee drawl. "Are you gittin' philosophical on me?" He ran his fingers through Sam's long, thick, wild red hair.

"Nope," Sam stated, "but I'm getting the oddest feeling."

"What's that?" Emma asked as she pushed another twig into the campfire.

"That the six of us were meant to be together and live happily ever after," Sam said. Then she planted a loud smack right on Pres's lips.

"I'll kiss to that," Carrie said, and she leaned over to kiss Billy.

"Kurt," Pres said, "you sure do know how to pick a camping spot."

"We aim to please," Kurt declared.

Right now, Emma thought as her friends continued to joke and goof around, *my life could not be better. I'm with people I love, with the guy I love, in a place that I love. What more could I want?*

Once again, her thoughts drifted back to the incredible circumstances that had helped her, Sam, and Carrie to become best friends, and her and Kurt to go from strangers to almost-marrieds to the brink of disaster and then back to boyfriend and girlfriend.

First, Carrie and Sam and me, Emma thought. *Each of us decides she wants to work as an au pair for a summer. Then we meet at the International Au Pair Convention in New York. Then we all get jobs here on Sunset Island! I'm working for the Hewitt family, who are the nicest; Sam's stuck with Dan Jacobs and his impossible fourteen-year-old twins; and Carrie's working for a rock star and his family!*

I'd never even have met them anywhere else but here, Emma told herself. *Not Sam, the wild and crazy tall girl with the wild and crazy red hair, who never fails to check out the guys wherever she goes and who was raised on a farm in Kansas! Not down-to-earth Carrie, with her pediatrician parents back in New Jersey and her ambitions to be a photojournalist.*

And they'd never have met me, Emma ruminated. *Not the girl Sam calls the Ice Princess because I'm rich, blond, petite, and blue-eyed and wear designer clothes.*

But now we're best friends, Emma thought. *And they are the closest and most important friends I've ever had in my life. We're here on fabulous Sunset Island, the famous resort island in Casco Bay off the coast of Portland, Maine. In the fall I have a zillion decisions to make, and I never, ever want this summer to end. What am I going to do when it's over?*

"Hey, Emma," Kurt whispered softly to her. "What are you thinking so hard about?"

Startled, Emma jumped. She glanced around and saw that Billy and Carrie were involved in a whispering conversation of their own, and that Sam and Pres were kissing again, oblivious to everyone else.

Emma smiled and sat up, hugging her knees to her chest. "Oh, just everything," she said softly.

"Good thing to be thinking about," Kurt replied, scootching over next to Emma and putting his left arm around her. "Chilly?"

"No," Emma answered softly, "but don't move your arm."

"What do you think of Dry Island?" Kurt asked, making a sweeping gesture at their surroundings.

"I love it!" Emma said. "Do we really have to go back tomorrow?"

The six of them had motored over to tiny Dry Island—so named because the island had no natural source of water—in a couple of Boston Whaler outboard boats earlier that day. All three girls had managed to get the weekend off from their jobs, and were free until Sunday night.

Kurt, who had grown up on Sunset Island, was the one who had organized the expedition; a couple of Maine lobstermen he knew had dropped them off, along with a large tent, camping equipment, and lots of water.

Dry Island was about three miles from the east end of Sunset Island, and Emma could just make out some of the lights flickering on the island she called home for the summer.

It does feel like home, Emma realized, looking out at the lights. *It feels more like home than Boston ever did.*

"You'd better hope my friends come back and pick us up tomorrow," Kurt joshed, brushing his light brown hair out of his eyes.

"You mean they might not show up?" Carrie asked.

"Good," Sam murmured. "I didn't want to go back, anyway."

"The last group my friends brought over

here to go camping got marooned when the guys forgot about them," Kurt said.

"Are you serious?" Emma asked skeptically.

Kurt smiled. "Believe that," he said, "and I've got some oceanfront property in Arizona to sell you." He pulled Emma into his arms.

"Right now," Emma said softly, "I'm ready to buy it, for the right price."

"How's this?" Kurt asked. He kissed her softly.

"I don't know," Emma whispered. "I'll think about your offer."

"I'll bid again," Kurt said, his deep blue eyes shining in the firelight. And when he kissed her this time, the kiss seemed to go on forever, and Emma felt as luminous as the stars that twinkled down on them.

"Well, good morning," Kurt said as Emma approached him. He was standing on the rocky beach, casting a fishing lure into the eddies of the incoming tide.

"Hi." Emma smiled warmly and gave Kurt a quick kiss.

"How'd you sleep?" Kurt asked.

Emma stretched to get the kinks out of her muscles. "You ought to know. Your sleeping bag was right next to mine."

"You snore," Kurt said.

"I do not!" Emma cried, playfully hitting Kurt's arm.

"Okay, I lied," Kurt said with a laugh. "But Billy snores something fierce!"

"I know, I heard him," Emma said with a smile. "Maybe next time we should try three separate tents instead of one big one."

"Hmmm, privacy, I like that idea," Kurt agreed.

"Did you catch anything?" she inquired, looking out at the water.

"Just a sculpin," Kurt replied.

"Never heard of it."

"Watch," Kurt said. He reeled the diamond-shaped lure up to the tip of his fishing rod, and slung it out toward the left. Then he started reeling fast. Instantly the rod doubled over. Kurt winked at Emma and kept on reeling. Moments later he pulled a fish up out of the water.

"Yuck!" Emma exclaimed. "That's the ugliest fish I've ever seen." Covered with

8

bumps, and with protruding eyes and big flapping fins, the fish struggled to free itself from the hook.

"I'm sure he doesn't think you're too pretty either, though I don't imagine he has very good taste in girls. Want to take it off the hook?" Kurt asked, a twinkle in his eye as he held the fish out to Emma.

"I'll pass," Emma said daintily, sitting down. Kurt took hold of the sculpin, unhooked it, and tossed it back into the murky green ocean.

"Enough fishing for one day," Kurt declared. "What time is it? You eat breakfast?"

"Almost eleven," Emma answered. "And yes, I ate."

"How was it?" Kurt queried.

"Don't let Sam get near a fry pan." Emma grimaced. "And next time, pack some tea for me."

Kurt sat down next to Emma, and together they stared off into the distance, each lost for the moment in private thoughts and dreams.

I can't believe that earlier this summer we weren't even talking to each other, Emma thought. *We almost lost each other forever. We both made a lot of mistakes. But I really do believe Kurt's changed, and so have I.*

"It's amazing we're here," Kurt said quietly, "after, well . . . after . . . you know."

"Not just us," Emma said. She brought her knees up to her chin and wrapped her arms around her jean-clad legs. A fairly stiff onshore breeze was starting to blow. "Billy and Carrie, too."

Earlier that summer, Billy's father had had a terrible accident in his auto-body shop in Seattle, and Billy had had to leave Sunset Island to go home to help out. Leaving the island had meant not only that he had to leave Carrie behind, but also that he had to leave his band, Flirting With Danger, for which he was the lead singer and which he had started with Pres years before.

He only got back to the island a week or so ago, Emma realized with amazement.

"Sam and Pres, too, for that matter," Kurt noted. "That's pretty amazing. Considering her track record with guys."

Emma had to agree. Sam and Pres were

in the second summer of their on-again, off-again relationship, and Emma had to admit that the off-again times were almost always caused by Sam's flirting with other guys. Recently, though, her friend from Kansas had really started to act a lot more serious toward the Flirts's handsome bass player.

"We're the most amazing," Emma said softly, so softly that she could barely be heard over the ocean lapping at the nearby rocks.

"That's true," Kurt agreed. "I was a jerk."

Emma looked at him with surprise. "Do you really believe that?"

Kurt nodded. "I just couldn't accept the fact that you're rich and I'm poor. I really gave you hell over it."

"I made a lot of mistakes, too," Emma said. "I never should have said I'd marry you when I wasn't ready to."

Kurt grinned at her. "So, here we are, older and wiser, right?"

"I think so," Emma said.

"My father thinks I'm an idiot," Kurt said matter-of-factly.

Emma groaned. Kurt's father, a rough-hewn Mainer with an inherent dislike for summer people, and particularly for multimillionaire summer people like Emma, had always been tough for her to deal with. After she and Kurt had had their terrible split-up earlier in the summer, Kurt's dad had even sent her a vicious letter accusing her of purposefully having taken advantage of his son.

That was so terrible, Emma recalled with a shudder. *I made some big mistakes, but he had no right to accuse me of those things, either!*

"What do you think?" Emma asked.

"I think it's not so easy for me to be at home now," Kurt declared. He ran his fingers over the two-day growth of beard on his face. "You know my dad—he doesn't say much. He just looks at me with those cold eyes of his, but I know what he's thinking. It's no picnic."

"Well, my parents, as you know, are no picnic, either," Emma pointed out.

She thought about her mother, Katerina, who insisted that everyone call her Kat, who tried desperately to be Emma's best friend instead of her mother.

Not that she even makes a good friend, Emma realized. *She only pays attention to me when she feels like it, and she doesn't feel like it all that often. Anyway, these days she's much too busy with her new romance with my father, her ex-husband!*

This thought made Emma laugh out loud.

"What's so funny?" Kurt asked her as he picked up a couple of pebbles and started juggling them with his left hand.

"I was just thinking about my parents," Emma explained. "I mean, in some ways, they're like us. They're giving each other a second chance."

"Their parents aren't giving them hell for it," Kurt pointed out. "If you'd like to come live with my dad while I go live at the Hewitts' house, I wouldn't argue you out of it."

"No, thanks," Emma declared.

"It doesn't matter," Kurt commented, standing up. He reached down for Emma with his right hand and pulled her up.

"It doesn't?"

"No," Kurt said as he began leading Emma down off the rocks. "I've just got to put up with it until the end of the summer."

"And then what?" Emma asked him.

"Then it's the Air Force Academy," Kurt replied. "I start in early September. You know that."

"Of course," Emma said dully. *Although I try not to think about it,* she added to herself.

"It's what you wanted," Kurt reminded her. "You said that we're too young to make a commitment, that we should both be pursuing our own lives."

"You're right," Emma agreed, trying to sound casual. "The Air Force Academy will be great for you. And I need another year of college before the Peace Corps will accept me so that I can go to Africa." That was Emma's dream. But when she'd applied, the Peace Corps had told her she needed at least one more year of college.

"Africa," Kurt echoed.

"Right," Emma said.

She looked at him sideways. *This is where we got into trouble before, she real-*

ized. Kurt was so afraid I'd go to the other side of the world and our relationship would end. But if we love each other, if we really love each other . . .

"Let's just live for the present," Kurt said softly, as if he were reading Emma's thoughts.

"I love you," she said huskily, and pulled Kurt to her for a passionate kiss.

But even as she was kissing him she felt the cold dread of what might happen to them when the leaves began to fall from the trees.

TWO

"Yuck," little Katie Hewitt said to Emma as she looked out the big picture window in the Hewitts' living room for about the eightieth time in the last hour. "It's still raining. I really, really hate rainy days. There's nothing to do. It's boring." She cuddled Snow White, her white kitten, then put her down on the floor.

"Yeah," her older brother Wills agreed. "It's boring. Really boring."

Emma sighed and looked at the wall clock. *Only eleven in the morning, and it's pouring out,* she thought. *What am I going to do to keep these kids occupied? Jane and Jeff Hewitt won't get home until seven*

17

tonight. This day is shaping up to be a disaster.

She looked outside again herself. The incessant rain showed no signs of letting up.

If anything, Emma thought, *it's getting worse. It's a monsoon out there.*

It was the Monday after the camping trip and Emma was back on the job as au pair for the Hewitt kids, Ethan, Wills, and little Katie. Katie was sweet most of the time, but recently she'd been going through a bratty stage. Emma had no idea why, unless it was because of the death of her beloved pet dog, whose name actually *was* Dog. The new kitten had been picked out as a replacement, but Emma knew the little girl still missed her old pet.

"Can I go play with Ethan and Dixie?" Katie asked, kicking her legs against the couch.

Twelve-year-old Ethan was in the kitchen playing Scrabble with Dixie Mason. Ethan and Dixie were both counselors-in-training at Club Sunset Island, the day camp that had recently opened at the Sunset Country Club. Dixie was Ethan's first girlfriend.

They're so cute together, Emma thought. *Dixie is a sweetheart, and she's really smart. She wants to be an astronaut, and she's bright enough to do it!*

"You can't play Scrabble," Wills told his sister. "You can't spell."

"I can, too," Katie insisted.

"Can not!"

"Can, too!"

"Not!"

"Too!"

"Give it a rest, you two!" Emma exclaimed, holding her hands over her ears.

Katie threw her brother a nasty look and then kicked him in the shin.

"Hey!" Wills yelled. "Cut it out!"

"Why did today have to be the day that the septic tank at the club decided to fail?" Emma said with a sigh. "I can't even take you guys there."

"The Weather Channel says it's gonna rain all day and all night," Katie declared. "I heard it."

"That sucks," Wills groaned.

"Yeah," Katie agreed.

"No, it's good," Emma said, trying to get the little girl to look on the bright side. "It's good for the flowers in your mom's garden."

"It's boring. I'm gonna go watch MTV," Katie announced, and then looked up at Emma expectantly, a somewhat defiant look on her face.

Great, Emma thought. *The kid is testing me. Katie knows very well that her mother wants me to limit the amount of TV the kids watch. And lately Katie doesn't want to do anything but watch MTV.*

"Katie knows we're not supposed to be watching TV," Wills reminded Emma, giving her a superior look. "Mom said so."

"These are . . . um . . . extenuating circumstances," Emma said, finally making up her mind.

"What?" Katie asked, totally puzzled.

"It means it's okay this once," Emma translated. "But watch upstairs so you don't disturb Ethan and Dixie."

"They might be kissing," Wills said, making a face.

"If they're gonna kiss, I wanna go watch!" Katie exclaimed.

"You may go watch MTV upstairs for a

half hour," Emma said firmly. "And no spying on your brother."

"Hurray!" Katie practically screamed with happiness. Then she did some very basic hip-hop dance moves. "Yo! MTV raps!" She bopped out of the room and up the stairs into her parents' bedroom, where seconds later Emma could hear the sound of hip-hop music blasting.

"Mom's not gonna like it," Wills warned.

"I'm willing to risk it," Emma said. "Why don't you go next door to Stinky's?" she suggested. Stinky Stein was Wills's best friend.

"He's at the dentist's," Wills said. "I guess I could play video games."

"Hey, turn it down up there!" Emma heard Ethan yell from the kitchen. But the music stayed at the same volume. Then Emma heard a bang as Ethan slammed shut the sliding door between the kitchen and the hallway.

If I can survive this day, Emma thought, *I can survive anything.*

"So," Emma said brightly to Wills. "You were going to go play video games, right?"

Wills nodded and got up slowly. "Tetris, I

21

guess." He walked over to the coffee table and picked up his Gameboy.

Aware that this was the first time the entire morning that all three kids were busy and quiet, Emma took a second to take the cordless phone into Jane and Jeff's home law office—they were both attorneys—and call Sam.

"Jacobs Mortuary," one of the twins answered in a loud voice. "You kill 'em, we chill 'em!"

"Hi," Emma said, ignoring the sick joke, "it's Emma. Is Sam there?"

"Hi, Emma, it's Becky. Just a sec. She's down in the walk-in freezer. *Yo, Sam! It's for you!*"

Emma heard the sound of the phone being set down and then picked up again a few seconds later.

"I'm having the day from hell, so be nice to me or else," Sam threatened. "Who is this?"

Emma laughed. "It's me. And what if it turned out I was your employer?"

"I wouldn't have cared," Sam said simply. "I hope they get the septic tank at the club fixed soon, otherwise I'm going to have to jump in it and do the repair job by myself."

Emma laughed again, settling back in Jane's office chair. "Do you have plans for tonight?"

"I didn't. Until now," Sam quipped. "Play Café, nine o'clock? That is, if I survive."

"That's good for me," Emma said.

"Me, too," said Becky on the extension.

"You're not invited," Sam snapped, "and what are you doing listening in on my phone call?"

"Well, you never told me to hang up," Becky rationalized. "Hey, Emma, will Kurt be there?"

"I don't know yet," Emma replied.

"You guys are together again, huh?" Becky asked.

"Excuse me," Sam said in an even voice, "but are you under the impression that someone invited you to be in on this conversation?"

"No, but—" Becky began.

"Then hang up the phone!" Sam screeched.

"Oh, take a chill pill, why don't you," Becky groused, but she hung up the phone.

"How do I stand it?" Sam asked Emma.

Ethan came marching into the office. "Emma, Katie is playing MTV so loud the walls are vibrating."

"Ask her to turn it down," Emma said.

"I already did. She told me rap music is supposed to be really loud and I'm too old to appreciate it," Ethan reported with disgust.

Emma laughed. "I'll go talk to her in a minute."

"Kids," Ethan grumbled, and walked away.

"Hey, you still there?" Sam called into the phone.

"Sorry," Emma said. "We're having a tough day around here. Listen, can you call Carrie? It's pretty crazy here."

"No prob," Sam replied. "A pleasure. As long as I don't have to talk to Becky or Allie, the fourteen-year-old nightmares, I'll talk to anyone!"

"They're giving you a hard time?"

"Nahhh," Sam said sarcastically. "Here's their latest scheme. They want to pose nude for a centerfold. Together."

"Oh, come on," Emma said with a laugh.

24

"They're not serious. They just say things like that to upset you."

"You think so?" Sam said. "Even as we speak they are up in their room trying on bikinis and posing for shots with the instant camera."

"Are you going to tell Mr. Jacobs?" Emma asked.

"I haven't decided yet, " Sam said. "Anyway, I'll see you later at the Play Café. Wish me luck surviving until then. Bye!"

"Bad day?" Carrie asked as Emma slid into the booth that she and Sam had already commandeered in the Play Café, the girls' favorite hangout.

Emma was completely soaked just from the walk from the parking spot she'd found a block away. Carrie untied the sweatshirt she was wearing knotted around her waist and handed it to her friend.

"Thank God for small favors," Emma said, toweling off her hair.

"Don't thank God," Sam quipped. "Thank Carrie Alden."

Carrie punched Sam playfully in the arm.

"Great outfit. Classy," Sam noted, taking in Emma's jeans and Goucher College T-shirt.

"Even I couldn't dress up on a day like today," Emma said, poking gentle fun at her own tendency to dress in expensive clothes.

"As you can see," Sam said, "*I* decided to dress for the occasion." She got up and spun around playfully, holding her arms out like a model.

"Sam," Emma declared, "only you could make a fashion statement out of a raincoat."

Sam was wearing a see-through slicker with red plastic bands around her bust and hips. Underneath that she wore long underwear and her red cowboy boots.

"Thank you," Sam said regally. "I'll take that as a compliment."

"Bad day?" Carrie repeated her earlier question.

"Oh, sorry, Carrie," Emma said when she realized she hadn't answered her friend before. "The worst. Worse than that, even. You?"

"A new low in the art of au pairing."

Carrie smiled. "Ian actually tied Chloe to a chair while I was on the phone with Sam."

"Every minute a fresh hell," Sam said. "I actually had to call the police!"

"No!" Emma exclaimed.

"But yes. I wanted to find out whether in the state of Maine killing two fourteen-year-old girls is a capital offense," Sam explained.

"What did the officer say?" Carrie asked, her lips twitching.

"'Not if you're their babysitter today, ma'am,'" Sam said, deadpan. Her friends laughed hard.

"What did you decide to do about the photo session?" Emma asked. She quickly filled Carrie in on what Sam had told her about the twins' plan to be the world's youngest centerfolds.

"I confiscated the film and the camera," Sam said. "They're ready to kill me. But I figured it was better than having to tell their father." She looked around the café. "It's dead in here tonight."

The Play Café, which was basically jam-packed every night of the week, whether it was a weekend or a weeknight, was barely half full. Even the high-volume video monitors, which usually blasted out current rock videos, seemed to have been turned down to a quieter level.

"We're the only three idiots who'd be out on a night like this." Carrie grinned.

"I had to escape," Sam said. "I was forced. Anyway, let's talk about something besides obnoxious kids. I've already ordered a double plate of nachos and a pitcher of diet Pepsi. So, Emma-bo-bemma, how's your love life? Did you and Kurt do the wild thing out on the rocks yesterday morning?"

"Sounds uncomfortable!" Carrie said with a laugh.

"Well, they could have stood up," Sam mused. "I've heard that it's possible."

"Sam!" Carrie scolded, shaking her head ruefully.

"I'm just curious," Sam chortled. "Emma would tell us. Wouldn't you, Emma?"

"Probably," Emma admitted. "But the truth is no, we didn't do the wild thing. You know what I decided."

"To wait until you're married," Sam said, rolling her eyes. "*Bor*-ing!"

"She didn't say *you* had to," Carrie pointed out.

"Good," Sam said mischievously. "Because I'm never getting married. And I do not intend to go to my grave without doing everything. And I do mean everything!"

Just then their waitress—a young black-haired woman they'd never seen there before—arrived with the nachos and diet Pepsi. She poured everyone a glassful, asked if they wanted anything else, and slunk away.

"The turnover in here is amazing," Sam commented. "It seems as if there's a new waitress every time we come in." She reached for a nacho and took a huge bite. "Serious yum," she announced. She turned to Emma. "So if you and the big guy didn't do you-know-what yesterday, what did you do?"

"Actually, Kurt and I had an interesting talk out on the rocks," Emma confided.

"About what?" Carrie asked, sipping her soda.

Emma filled her friends in on the conversation that she'd had with Kurt the morning before, especially the part about the problems that Kurt had been having with his dad.

"I think he'll get over it," Carrie said. "Kurt's dad is basically a good guy."

"You'd think he'd be thrilled that his kid was in love with a babe with major bucks," Sam said, licking some cheese off her pinky.

"Oh, Sam," Emma sighed, "you know how proud that family is. It would be much easier for Kurt's dad to accept me if I were dirt poor!"

"Gruesome thought," Sam said with a shudder.

"So what's going on with you two?" Emma asked Sam. "Fair's fair, isn't it?"

"I guess," Sam mumbled, her mouth full of nachos. "Anyway, I finally slept with Presley Travis."

Emma almost dropped her glass. "You did?" she exclaimed.

"Sure," Sam said easily. "In a tent with four other people. Saturday night. You were there. And, I might add, it was totally delicious."

"But you didn't—"

"I just *said* you were there," Sam repeated. "You think I'm going to go for it the first time with two other couples in the same tent?" She looked over at Carrie. "I did wake up in the middle of the night, though, and I just happened to notice that you and Billy were nowhere to be seen."

Carrie smiled. Earlier that summer, before he had to leave to go home to Seattle, she and Billy had made love for the first time.

"We might have gone off by ourselves for a little while," Carrie allowed.

Well, why shouldn't they? Emma thought. *They've been in a long-term, committed relationship for two years. They had AIDS tests. Carrie uses birth control and Billy uses condoms. Even if Carrie's decision isn't what my decision is, I respect her for acting like an adult about it. Actually, I think we've both made the right decisions for each of us.*

"You mean in the middle of the night the two of you—" Sam began.

"Sam," Emma interrupted gently, "that's private."

"*Donnez-moi une* break!" Sam snorted. "I want details!"

"Not if you don't want to," Emma told Carrie.

"It's not that big a deal," Carrie stated, taking a sip of her drink. "He's back. He's been back for a week. Yes, we've slept together again. And we've also been to the movies, gone hiking, been out to dinner . . . you know what I mean."

"Go back to the part where you slept together, because I know there was no actual sleeping involved."

Carrie leaned forward. "Sam," she said to her friend, "you know it's no accident that you haven't slept with Pres yet. Just like it's no accident that Emma hasn't slept with Kurt."

I love Carrie, Emma thought. *She's not afraid to tell us the truth. Am I ever going to have that kind of courage?*

Sam smiled weakly, and then picked up a nacho and chewed on it thoughtfully. "Busted," she admitted.

"You should be proud of sticking to your guns," Carrie said. "If you're not ready to have sex, then you shouldn't do it. End of report."

"It's completely an individual decision," Emma agreed.

Carrie nodded. "What's right for me isn't necessarily right for you. And vice versa."

"Yeah," Sam said, "and I'm just not ready."

"That's okay," Carrie said, "because—"

"But I've got to tell you," Sam interrupted her, "I'm dying to know when I will be!" She reached for another nacho. "Maybe this fall Pres and I will take a road trip or something. Maybe then—"

"Don't talk about the fall," Emma said quickly.

Her friends stared at her.

"It's just that Kurt's going to the Air Force Academy in the fall," Emma explained. "I'm going back to college. And . . . well, it scares me."

"Me, too," Carrie admitted. "Billy says there's a chance he'll have to go back to Seattle. Then what? I'll be back at Yale. . . ."

"You guys could just drop out of college, like I did!" Sam suggested.

"And what?" Emma asked sarcastically. "Follow Kurt to the Air Force Academy?"

"Follow Billy to Seattle?" Carrie added with equal sarcasm.

"Okay, so it's not a good idea," Sam admitted. "I guess there's only one solution. This summer just can never end!"

THREE

Emma woke up the next morning to the sound of hard rain pelting against her window.

"Oh, no," she groaned, and covered her head with the pillow. "Not another day when the kids can't go outside."

She moved the pillow and looked at the clock on her nightstand. It was 9:50. *Jeff and Jane must have let me sleep in because of the weather,* she realized. *That was nice of them. Thank goodness they're here. I couldn't take another day like yesterday.*

She took a quick shower and dressed in some jeans and an off-white cable-knit sweater, then ran downstairs, expecting the worst.

But in contrast to the previous day of misery, when Jeff and Jane had been working, what greeted her was a picture of family harmony.

The entire Hewitt family was sitting around the kitchen table, playing Parcheesi.

"You slept late," Jeff Hewitt said to her, offering her the sixth chair at the table. "You want to play?"

"No, thanks," Emma said politely, going over to the stove and pouring herself a cup of tea from the teapot resting on it. "It was really nice of you to let me sleep."

"Were you out with Kurt?" Katie asked eagerly.

"No, sweetie," Emma replied. "I was with Sam and Carrie."

"Kurt is your boyfriend again, right?" Katie questioned.

"Yes," Emma replied. She took the tea to the table and sat down.

"That's good," Katie decided. "I missed him."

"Me, too," Emma said softly. She took a

sip of her hot tea while Wills took his turn at the game. "I guess the septic tank at the club is still broken, right?"

"No camp," Wills stated matter-of-factly."

Jane Hewitt pointed to the sky. "If it keeps raining like this, they'll never be able to fix it," she said.

"Dixie called and told me there's, like, practically a river running past the Mason's house," Ethan told Emma.

Dixie was staying with Molly Mason, her cousin, for the summer, which meant she was living in the same house as their friend Darcy Laken. It was a huge old house on a hill, decorated in horror chic in honor of the Masons' love for the horror movies they wrote for a living.

"Lots of people are going to be flooded," Jeff observed, looking outside at the storm.

"This is not exactly what the Sunset Island Chamber of Commerce had in mind," Jane added, reaching for the dice to take her turn.

"Any word on when it's supposed to stop?" Emma asked hopefully.

"The Weather Channel says this afternoon," Katie chimed in. "Then sunny, temperature in the low eighties."

"My daughter's going to be a meteorologist," Jeff joked.

"Maybe you'll have camp tomorrow, then," Emma observed, taking another small sip of tea. *Please, please, please,* she added to herself, crossing her fingers superstitiously under the table.

"Hey!" Jeff Hewitt exclaimed, his eyes gleaming. "I just got a great idea!"

"What?" Jane asked. She moved one of her red markers around the game board.

"You remember our trip to Seattle right after college, just before I went into VISTA?" Jeff asked his wife.

"Uh-huh," Jane said. Her marker landed on the spot where one of Ethan's green markers lay. "Ha, sent you back to home," she said, moving the green marker.

"Bummer," Ethan said with a sigh.

"Do you remember that time it rained so much that we went—"

Jane looked over at her husband. "No way, honey," she said with a laugh.

"Why not?" Jeff pressed.

"Because—"

38

"They can take showers later," Jeff insisted.

"What, Dad?" Ethan asked eagerly.

"Yeah, what?" Wills piped up.

"Whatever it is, I get to do it, too," Katie said.

"See?" Jeff said. "The kids are enthusiastic and they don't even know what it is yet!"

Jane laughed and wagged her finger at her husband. "You are the biggest kid of all."

"Right," he agreed. "So, you up for it?"

"What is it? What is it?" Katie yelled with excitement.

Jane sighed, but she couldn't keep the smile off her face. "As long as all I have to do is supervise."

"It's a deal," Jeff said. He got up and leaned over to kiss his wife on the cheek.

"I have to know what it is!" Katie squealed. "Am I gonna be on MTV?"

"You are so lame," Wills told her. "Why would you be on MTV?"

"Because I'm cute and I'm a good singer," Katie said, sticking her tongue out at Wills.

"You're four years old!" Wills said with exasperation.

"So? Haven't you ever heard of a child star?"

"You're really turning into a brat," Ethan told his sister.

"I'm not a brat! You're a brat!" Katie insisted. "I'm bad, like Salt 'N' Pepa!"

"Uh, Daddy dearest," Jane said mildly, "now would be a good time to unveil your big surprise before these kids get any nastier to each other."

Jeff folded his arms. "Before I tell you guys the plan, I want you to know I expect you to treat each other with respect."

"But Dad—" Wills began.

"This is not open to debate," Jeff said. "Have I made myself clear?"

"Okay," Wills said with a sigh.

"Son?" Jeff asked Ethan.

"Sure, Dad," Ethan agreed.

"And you, young lady?" Jeff asked, turning to Katie.

"But Daddy—"

"I mean it, Katie," Jeff said firmly.

"Okay, Daddy. I'm sorry."

"Well done," Jane said, tipping her coffee cup to her husband.

Jeff grinned at her, then turned back to his kids. "Okay, here's the deal, you guys. Go put on your oldest clothes. And bring down towels."

"A lot of towels," Jane chimed in, pushing her chair away from the table. "The beach towels, not the good ones."

"And a change of clothes," Jeff added, helping the kids put away the Parcheesi game.

"Wear old clothes? And bring something to change into? We're going out?" Ethan asked dubiously. "It's like, completely pouring outside!"

"You in, Emma?" Jeff asked.

Emma was stumped. "In for what?" she asked.

"It's a new Olympic sport," Jeff replied. "We're going mud-sliding!"

"This is awesome!" Ethan Hewitt yelled at the top of his lungs as he stood at the top of the tallest hill in Sunset Island's municipal park.

"Totally awesome!" his kid brother, Wills, chimed in.

"Awesome awesome!" screamed Katie, not wanting to be left out.

"Here I go!" shouted Ethan, and Emma watched as Ethan took six running strides, and then launched himself on his belly. He slid downhill over the close-cropped and muddy grass at almost unbelievable speed, not stopping until he came to the very bottom of the steep hill.

"How about you, Emma?" Jeff Hewitt asked. He was standing next to her.

"I'll pass," Emma said, and pulled the yellow rain slicker she was wearing even closer around her. Jeff and the kids all seemed to be having a blast. Jane had decided to stay home and make some homemade soup for everyone to eat when they got back. It was still raining cats and dogs, and there wasn't another soul in the park.

"Guess I'm alone, then," Jeff said innocently. "Okay, time for some kiddy bowling!" He took three enormous strides of his own and launched himself down the hill. The kids yelled with glee as, at the bottom of the hill, Jeff barreled directly but gently into them, knocking them to the ground like human bowling pins in an outdoor alley. The whole Hewitt clan rolled around in the mud like a bunch of cavorting otters.

"Daddy, you're all dirty!" Katie squealed with delight, plopping down in the mud next to her father.

"So are you!" Jeff said, splashing some mud at his daughter.

"So?" Katie said. "I don't care! It's so fun!" She threw her arms around her father and hugged him. Then Ethan and Wills tackled their dad from behind, until they were all rolling around in the mud, laughing their heads off.

He's the greatest father, Emma thought, a little wistfully, hugging herself to keep warm. *His kids love him so much. He's a grown-up, but he's not afraid to have fun. That's exactly the kind of thing that my father never did with me. Or my mother, for that matter. She would never have gone out in the rain to play with me. Not in a million years.*

Emma saw Jeff Hewitt stand and motion to her to come down the hill to where their van was parked. Emma slipped the small

43

camera she'd been using to snap pictures of the family adventure in her pocket and made her way gingerly down the hill.

When she got to the van, the Hewitts were all toweling off and changing into their other clothes.

"Can't I wear these home?" Katie asked as she surveyed her mud-covered jeans and T-shirt.

"I think Mom might object," Jeff observed, making a big pile of muddy clothes in the back of the van.

Soon the Hewitts and Emma were heading home. Jeff Hewitt snapped on the radio to help pass the time. Emma heard the announcer say something about an unexpected stock-market collapse, how investors were taking it on the chin.

"You and Mom own stock, don't you?" Ethan asked his dad.

"Some," Jeff said, stopping at a red light that could barely be seen through the pouring rain.

"So if the stock market falls, do we lose a lot of money?" Ethan asked his dad.

"No, son, it's okay," Jeff said. "We own

pretty conservative, safe stocks, and we don't own that many, anyway."

My parents do, Emma thought to herself, *but my father is too savvy ever to let a problem with the stock market affect his holdings. It's funny—I guess if you're rich enough, like me, or poor enough, like Kurt, a stock-market crash doesn't hurt you at all.*

After that, she didn't give it another thought.

The entire Hewitt family, Emma included, was gathered around the television set, watching the evening news. The lead story was about the financial markets.

The stock market had crashed badly that day, losing about ten percent of its value. Late in the afternoon, it had become a real panic as investors looked to unload their shares, no matter the price. And some of the international markets, such as those in Hong Kong and the Philippines, did even worse than the New York exchange.

"Are you sure we're okay, Dad?" Ethan asked anxiously.

"I promise," Jeff said. He put his arm around his son. "The stock market can be volatile. Your mom and I make very careful investments."

Just then the telephone rang. "I'll get it," Emma said, since she was expecting a call from Sam. She went to the phone in the kitchen and answered it.

"Hewitt residence, Emma Cresswell speaking," she said in her usual well-bred voice.

"Emma, sweetheart, it's your father!" said the voice at the other end of the line. "I'm so happy to talk to you. I was afraid I wouldn't be able to reach you."

Dad, Emma thought. *I haven't talked to him in a couple of weeks. I know he's gone back to living in Boston, so he can be closer to my mother, but he's not living with her—he's got his own apartment there.*

Then a sudden wave of concern came over her. Earlier that summer, Emma's dad, Brent Cresswell, a self-made millionaire who had his own investment-advising firm, had been hospitalized because of a heart attack. Actually, he had almost died; he'd had to be flown by helicopter to Maine

Medical Center, and had gotten there just in the nick of time.

Oh, no, Emma thought in a panic. *It's his heart; he's having trouble with his heart again.*

"Dad, are you okay?" Emma asked quickly, grabbing the phone tightly. "Is your heart okay?"

"I'm fine, Emma," Brent said briskly, but Emma could hear a note of strain in his voice.

"You don't sound fine," Emma said anxiously.

"My heart's fine," Brent answered, with a bitter little laugh. "After the day I've had, I can assure you that my heart is just fine. It's gone through the test of fire."

Emma sat down in one of the kitchen chairs. Obviously her father was referring to the stock market's problems that day. Not only was he heavily invested in the stock market, but as a financial planner, he helped his clients decide how to invest.

It's amazing how little I think about what he does day to day, Emma mused. *I mean, I just take it all for granted. But Dad must have lots of people who depend on him for advice. Today must have been horrible for him. And I didn't even think of calling him. I am so selfish sometimes.*

"It was the stock-market crash," Emma murmured. "I'm really sorry. Was it bad for your clients?"

"It wasn't good," Brent replied, that strain still in his voice.

"It'll get better," Emma ventured. She unconsciously played with a lock of her hair as she spoke.

"Maybe," Brent said tonelessly.

"Did a lot of your customers lose money today?" Emma asked, sure that was what he was so upset about.

"A lot of the *world* lost money today," Brent said with a sigh. "So yes, a lot of my customers lost money today. A *lot* of money."

"You're smart, Dad," Emma whispered. "You'll get it back for them."

Silence.

This is scaring me, Emma thought. *Why is he acting so strange?*

"Emma?"

"Yes, Daddy?"

Brent Cresswell cleared his throat. "My

48

customers weren't the only ones who lost money today. I—we—lost a lot, too."

"Good thing we have a lot," Emma quipped, trying to make a joke. She curled the phone cord around her fingers.

The whole conversation was making Emma wildly uncomfortable. *My family never talks about money,* Emma thought. *That's one of the subjects that is off-limits for the Cresswells. Money is something that's always just there.*

There was more silence on the other end of the phone.

"Dad, are you still there?"

"Yes," Brent replied.

"It'll get better, I guarantee it," Emma said, trying to cheer her father up.

Then Emma heard a sound she had never heard before in her life.

She heard Brent Cresswell crying.

"Emma," he mumbled through the sobs, "I let everyone down."

"No, you didn't, Dad!" Emma cried. "It's not your fault that the market crashed!"

"Emma," her father said, "you don't understand."

"Yes, I do," Emma said quickly, sure that

her father was just beating up on himself over something he couldn't control.

"No, you don't," Brent insisted. "Emma, I was invested in the Far East—Hong Kong. I couldn't even sell the shares today. Nothing! No one would make a market. Nothing!"

Emma felt a wave of fear come over her. "What . . . what are you saying, Dad?"

Emma's father composed himself. Emma could hear him inhale deeply and clear his throat. "I'm sorry I lost control, Emma."

"Don't worry about it, Dad—"

"You need to understand the situation," Brent said in a ragged voice. "I don't want to beat around the bush. I'm broke. There's a good chance that by next week I'll have to declare bankruptcy."

FOUR

"Your dad is really broke?" Sam asked, aghast. "As in no money?"

"That's what he told me," Emma replied.

"That's an amazing story," Carrie said, sitting up to spread some more suntan lotion on her legs, below the cutoff shorts she was wearing with a plain Yale T-shirt.

"Too bad it's true," Emma said ruefully. She'd just finished telling her friends the story of the phone call with her father the evening before.

"Wow, it's like something out of a movie," Sam commented, adjusting the straps on her swimsuit. She had on her newest bikini, a flesh-toned mesh number that made her look naked from far away.

"I wish it weren't true," Emma replied, adjusting her own white suit, which was a simple but expensive designer one-piece with high-cut legs. "It's horrible for him."

"Well, it's probably not such a biggie," Sam decided, reaching for Carrie's suntan lotion.

"How can you say that?" Carrie asked.

"Emma's mother will lend him what he needs," Sam said with a shrug. She squirted the suntan lotion on her long, tanned legs. "And then he'll earn more."

Finally, Sunset Island was having a nice day. As forecast, the two-day rainstorm had ended the previous afternoon, and the skies had been swept clear of clouds in less than an hour. The break in the weather had let the repair crew at the country club fix the septic system, and now, twenty-four hours later, Sam, Carrie, and Emma's lives were back to normal.

Basically back to normal, Emma thought. *As normal as can be when you know that one of your parents might have to declare bankruptcy!*

Club Sunset Island also had reopened, so the older kids the girls took care of were occupied again. This meant that Sam, Emma, and Carrie could finally hang out by the pool at the country club. In the meantime, little Chloe Templeton and Katie Hewitt were playing together in the kiddy pool.

"It isn't that simple," Emma tried to explain.

"Your mother has millions on top of her millions, right?" Sam queried. She adjusted her new leopard-print sunglasses on her nose.

"Right," Emma answered, "but—"

"And she and your dad are an item again, right?" Sam continued.

"Pretty much, but—"

"I rest my case," Sam declared. She settled down on her back, her hands under her head. "Just be glad it's not you who's broke."

"I am glad," Emma said truthfully.

Sam laughed. "Emma Cresswell without money, can you imagine it?"

"Not really," Carrie admitted.

"I'd be the same person," Emma said defensively.

"Yeah, right," Sam snorted. "You have absolutely no concept of what it's like to live like us mortals."

I wonder if she's right, Emma thought pensively. *Would I be different if I was poor?*

Sam sighed contentedly. "This is the life, huh? The sun feels heavenly."

"Hey," Carrie reminded her, "it's supposed to be your turn to watch Chloe and Katie for the next half hour. That was our deal. I'm the one who's sunbathing here."

"I'll use my au pair X-ray vision," Sam said lazily.

"What X-ray vision?" Emma asked.

"For example," Sam continued, her eyes closed behind her sunglasses, "I can see Katie and Chloe perfectly now."

"You can't," Carrie challenged her.

"Yes, I can," Sam replied blithely.

"So what are the kids doing?" Emma asked, getting into the spirit of it. "Tell us, Miss X-ray Vision."

"Right now Chloe's splashing Katie, and Katie is imitating Toni Braxton by singing into a tennis ball," Sam said, as easily as if she could see it with her own eyes.

And that was exactly what was happening in the kiddy pool.

"How could you know that?" Emma asked, amazed.

"Au pair sixth sense," Sam declared.

"Get out of here," Carrie said with a laugh.

"What can I tell you?" Sam retorted. "Kids are so predictable."

"Well, hi there," two guys said, walking over to the girls, who all looked up. One guy was tall and blond with a small goatee. The other was short and dark with the build of a weightlifter.

"Hi," Sam said brightly. "Do I know you?"

"No," the blond one said. "But we'd like to know you."

"Gee, thanks," Sam replied. "I can't blame you!"

The dark guy laughed. "My name's John and this is my buddy Allen. Listen, we were, like, on the other side of the pool and we thought you were naked."

"Me?" Sam screeched.

Allen nodded. "That bathing suit looks

like skin, you know? So we decided to come over here and see if you actually had anything on."

"Because clearly, foxy mama," John added, "you do have it *going* on." He rubbed his hands together with anticipation. His friend licked his lips.

"That's the cheesiest line I ever heard," Carrie told John.

"Right," Sam agreed. "I am not naked—what a shocker—and you two cheeseballs can take a hike."

"Forget her," Allen said with disgust. "She hasn't got enough under that bikini top to fill a Dixie cup, anyway."

Then, laughing hysterically, the two guys sauntered off.

"I have to go kill him," Sam said.

"Not worth it," Emma said.

"You know what really gets me?" Sam asked. "How, when someone wants to make you feel really awful, they just go for whatever it is you feel most insecure about."

"My thighs," Carrie muttered.

"My lack of hooters," Sam said with a

sigh. She turned to Emma. "What is it with you?"

"I . . . I don't know," Emma faltered.

"I hate you," Sam said. "There's nothing about you to make fun of. You're gorgeous and rich. You're even nice. Get me a gun, somebody, she doesn't deserve to live!"

Just then one of the young teen waiters—he couldn't have been more than sixteen—brought three tall glasses of iced tea and a big bag of Doritos over to the girls.

"You order anything?" Carrie asked Emma.

"No," Emma replied.

"You?" Carrie asked Sam.

"I know you'll find this hard to believe . . ." Sam began.

"But . . ." Carrie continued, not at all surprised that Sam, who had a bottomless pit for a stomach, would have ordered food for them despite their having eaten lunch only an hour or so beforehand.

". . . I didn't order a thing," Sam concluded.

"Sorry, but these aren't ours," Emma told the waiter politely.

"Yes, they are," the waiter corrected, setting the glasses of iced tea and the bag of chips down on the metal table near the girls.

"We didn't order them," Carrie repeated. "I'm sorry, you'll have to take them back."

"You're Sam Bridges, Carrie Alden, and Emma Dresswell?" he asked.

"Dresswell—that's great!" Sam hooted.

"Emma Cresswell," Emma corrected him automatically, sitting up on her chaise.

"Sorry," the young waiter said, grinning at Emma. "Someone ordered this stuff for you. Your names are on this. There's a note with them." He handed the girls an envelope, which Sam took. Then he turned away.

"It's us, all right," Sam said, reading the envelope.

"Emma's name is misspelled," Carrie noted.

"Big duh," Sam said, tearing the envelope open.

Inside, written in a florid, obviously female handwriting, was this note. All the girls leaned over and read it together, silently.

Sam, Carrie, and especially Emma Eusta Dresswell, who won't be able to afford to dress well for long—I ordered drinks for you because I know that Emma can't buy them for you anymore. Her dad had kind of a rough day yesterday, and in case you don't know, the markets are down another fifteen percent today. So enjoy, and use the other thing in this envelope to call someone who cares.

Sam looked inside the envelope again. At the bottom of it was a quarter.

"The she-devil from hell, I just know it," Sam moaned.

"Diana," Carrie sighed.

"It doesn't surprise me," Emma muttered. "She's capable of anything."

"She eats small children for breakfast," Sam observed. "And Lorell sprinkles the sugar on top."

The girls were referring to Diana De Witt, their archenemy on the island. Diana and her best friend, Lorell Courtland, seemed to exist only to make the lives of Sam, Emma, and Carrie totally miserable.

Diana and Emma had gone to boarding school in Switzerland together, but that connection just seemed to furnish Diana with even more ammunition to lob at her. And then, when Diana had been kicked out of Flirting With Danger, the band that she, Emma, and Sam sang backup for, the situation had gone from bad to worse.

Both of them were gorgeous: Diana with her chestnut curls, deep-set blue eyes, and perfectly aerobicized figure, and black-haired Lorell, who was raised in a rich family in Atlanta, with her light blue eyes and super-sugary Southern accent.

I can't believe that Kurt actually slept with Diana, Emma thought bitterly. *But that was a long time ago, and—*

"Don't look now," Sam said, sitting up in her chaise, "but look who's coming."

"Not—" Carrie started.

"Yep," Sam broke in, "the Bad Dream Team, live and in person."

Emma turned to the left, following Sam's eyes. Approaching them were Diana and Lorell, together.

As usual, they looked fantastic. Diana was wearing a copper and black one-piece suit with black fishnet in the middle, and Lorell had on a violet and white polka-dot bikini.

"I understand Diana sent y'all a present," Lorell drawled as she came closer.

"Nice of me." Diana grinned evilly.

"Gee, how rude of me, Diana," Sam said sourly. "I forgot to thank you for the iced tea."

"Oh, no need to thank me, Sam—" Diana began, but her words came to a screeching stop when Sam calmly reached over, took her glass of iced tea, and poured it directly onto the concrete deck next to her lounge chair.

Carrie and Emma laughed, and Emma could see that even Diana started to crack a grin.

"Two points for the stork from Kansas," Diana said to Sam. "But I'm glad that was your iced tea you were pouring out and not Emma's, because I have an idea that Emma's going to need the free food."

"Why don't you mind your own business?" Carrie asked, leaning forward on her chaise in order to confront Diana and Lorell.

Diana gave a short laugh. "My own business. That's the whole problem," she snorted.

"I'll say," Lorell echoed, dabbing with her toe at the little stream of iced tea that was now wending its way across the concrete toward her sandal-clad feet.

"What are you talking about?" Sam asked. "You're making even less sense than usual." As she talked she calmly picked up another of the glasses of iced tea and took a sip. When she set it down next to her, she deliberately tipped it over so it would spill in Lorell and Diana's direction.

This time they didn't notice.

"We'd explain it to you, but a girl from your background just couldn't understand, honey," Lorell said with fake sympathy.

"Emma," Diana said regally, stepping away from the chaises, "I'd really like to thank you."

"For what?" Emma asked.

"For having your father lose my family a ton of money," Diana spat.

"Talk about mindin' your business,"

Lorell cooed, still not noticing the new flood of tea. "Your daddy sure had some trouble mindin' other people's."

"The crash wasn't my father's fault!" Emma retorted hotly.

"The market just slumped," Carrie added, defending Emma.

"My father had money invested with your father's firm," Diana challenged.

"Fortunate—yuck!" Lorell exclaimed, gingerly stepping away from the cold tea that was threatening her toes. "As I was saying, fortunately Mr. De Witt got most of it out in time."

"It wasn't my father's—"

"Yes, it was," Diana said in a chilly voice. "He's supposed to be an investment advisor."

"Not an investment fool," Lorell chimed in.

"It wasn't his fault," Sam said, sticking up for Emma.

Diana opened her hand to reveal a penny. She flipped it into the air and caught it, then threw it carelessly a few feet away. "You probably ought to go after that, Miss Dresswell," Diana jeered. "It looks like you're going to need it."

"Curl up and die," Sam said with disgust. She lay back down on her lounger. "I mean it. The two of you are too boring for words."

"I'll second that," Carrie agreed, turning over onto her stomach.

"I don't see you acting so nonchalant," Diana observed, narrowing her eyes at Emma.

"Believe it or not," Emma said in an even voice, "I'm concerned about my father. And I don't happen to think making fun of people when they're down is hip, cool, or clever."

"Why, she's just so plucky and brave!" Lorell remarked sarcastically. "I for one am *so* impressed! Aren't you, Diana?"

"Give it a rest, Lorell," Diana said sharply, and she walked away, Lorell hurrying to catch up.

"Wow, what just happened there?" Carrie asked.

"I think I told Diana the truth without flinging an insult at her, and she backed down," Emma said incredulously.

"I-W-L," Sam intoned, not lifting her head up from the lounger.

"What's that stand for?" Emma asked.

"It won't last," Sam said. "Now someone hand me the free Doritos."

"I feel so bad for my father," Emma said to Kurt as she thoughtfully chewed on another fried clam.

"It must be rough for him," Kurt agreed.

"If only there was something I could do!" Emma exclaimed.

It was much later that evening. Emma had gotten off work at nine, when Jane and Jeff Hewitt came home from some political fund-raising dinner they'd been attending in Portland. Kurt had picked her up in his father's car, and together they'd driven to Rubie's Diner, down near the old fishermen's pier.

At first, Emma had been reluctant to go there—Rubie's was where she and Kurt had had their wedding rehearsal dinner, and that hadn't gone particularly well.

But Rubie herself—who was pretty much Kurt's adopted aunt—had come out herself to greet them, and threw her massive arms around Emma's neck to hug her.

"Good to see you back, sweetheart," she'd said.

"It's good to be back," Emma had said in a small voice.

Rubie had set Kurt and Emma up on the small table on the deck of her restaurant, overlooking the lobstermen's squat boats. Because there was no wind at all, the boats were anchored every which way in the water, instead of being neatly lined up with their bows pointing into the prevailing wind.

There was a bright full moon—so bright that Emma could read the Maine state registration numbers painted on the bows of the boats.

"There's not much you can do," Kurt pointed out.

"I know that," Emma said. "But I wish there were."

"I wish there were something you could do about *my* dad," Kurt said pensively, taking a sip from his glass of water.

"Problems?" Emma asked quietly.

"The usual," Kurt answered.

"Me," Emma said meekly.

"You," Kurt responded.

"Why does it have to be like this with your father?" Emma asked in a quiet voice.

"Maybe you ought to ask him that sometime," Kurt suggested.

Emma stared at him.

"I'm only kidding," Kurt continued.

"No," Emma said, "you're not."

"I am!" Kurt insisted.

"I *am* willing to talk to your father," Emma said, screwing up her courage.

"You are?"

"If he's willing to talk to me," she continued, reaching for one more fried clam.

"He isn't," Kurt summed up.

"What does he say to you?" Emma asked. *Not that I really want to know,* she thought. *I am sure all he says are hateful things about me, about how I'm ruining his son's life, how I hurt him once and I'll hurt him again.*

"You can imagine," Kurt said.

Emma sat in silence. She could imagine all too well.

"Look, it's only for the rest of the summer," Kurt reminded her.

Emma felt a stabbing sensation near her heart. "What do you mean?"

"I mean I won't be living with him in the fall," Kurt said. "What did you think I meant?"

That we wouldn't be together, Emma thought. "Oh, nothing," she murmured, playing with the straw in her drink.

Kurt reached for her hand. "Emma, after everything we've been through, I think our relationship can stand our being apart, don't you?"

"That's not what you used to say," Emma reminded him. "You said long-distance romances never work."

"Well, I've changed my mind," Kurt replied. "Anyway, we're here now, the night is perfect, and we're together. What more could we want?"

What more indeed? Emma thought.

But she couldn't figure out why she was shivering on such a warm night.

FIVE

"Go for it," Billy suggested.

Emma shook her head.

"Try it, Emma," Pres drawled.

"Yeah, give it a whirl," said Jake Fisher, the handsome drummer for Flirting With Danger, grinning at Emma.

"You can do it, girlfriend," Sam said supportively.

"I really don't want to," Emma finally said, feeling extremely uncomfortable.

"Of course you want to," Sam insisted. "Who wouldn't want a solo?"

"I just don't feel I can do it," Emma began.

"Hey, girl, you won't know until you've

tried, will you?" Pres urged, strapping his bass guitar around his neck.

Billy walked over to her and spoke quietly. "I know you can do it," he urged her.

"You don't need me to play," Jay Bailey, the keyboard player, encouraged her. "You sound great. So go for it."

It was the next afternoon, and the Flirts were all gathered at their big, ramshackle house in a quiet residential part of the island. They'd turned one of their rooms into a music studio, where the band rehearsed.

Because Katie Hewitt was with her mother in Portland for the day and Wills was at a friend's, Emma had been able to get away for a few hours to come to this rehearsal. But the last thing she had expected was for the band to decide that she should do a solo.

They're asking me to do the impossible! I'm not even that good a singer!

At the beginning of the rehearsal, Billy and Pres had approached Emma with an idea for a new arrangement of one of their songs. On the Flirts's big East Coast tour earlier in the year, Carrie had written a song called "No One Knows Love," on which Emma had sung lead at the Malcolm X Theater Center in Washington, D.C.

"It's called *a capella*," Jake said.

"No instruments," Billy translated. "Only your voice."

"Just at first," Pres said, "then we'll come in."

Now Emma turned to look at Sam and the other backup singer, Erin Kane. Erin was new with the band; she was a gorgeous, really sweet, full-figured girl with a fabulous voice and wild blond hair. She had replaced Diana, and everyone agreed it was a huge improvement.

"You two want to try this?" Emma asked shyly.

Erin and Sam both nodded vigorously. "You're the one out front," Sam quipped. "So—"

"What do we have to worry about?" Erin finished Sam's joke for her. "Besides," she added, "isn't this the same tune you sang on tour before I was with the group?"

"Only once," Emma said. "And the arrangement was so different, it was so much easier—"

"You can do this," Pres told her firmly. "You don't even know what a good singer you are, Emma."

"Because I'm not," she said, laughing faintly.

"I love it when she suffers from lack of confidence," Sam said, sticking her hair up in a ponytail to get it off her neck. "It makes her seem almost human!"

"Don't tease her, now," Erin said, nudging Sam in the ribs.

"Right," Emma agreed. "I'm fragile." She took a deep breath. "Okay, I'll do it." She smoothed some nonexistent wrinkles out of the sleeveless white linen shirt she was wearing with her white jeans. "But I'm not saying it's going to be any good."

"Just take the first verse nice and slow," Billy instructed, tuning the G string on his guitar.

"Don't rush the tempo," Jake advised. "Kind of lay it back."

"Then when Erin and Sam come in on the harmonies you can get into a more rhythmic groove," Jay suggested.

"Please, no more instructions!" Emma said, putting her hands over her ears. "I'm too nervous for any of it to register!"

She walked slowly to the lone mike set up in front of the band and took a deep breath.

"Whenever you're ready," Billy said. "I'll count you in, but then you can take it how you like it, nice and free."

Emma said a quick prayer, basically the same prayer she'd said before she had sung Carrie's song in Washington, with one twist—*Please, God, don't let me ruin this. Let me be good, and thank You for not giving me a roomful of strangers now!*—and began to sing softly into the microphone.

No one knows love the way that I do.
No one knows how to play it so cool.
So who can I trust? Where should I be?
No one knows love, especially me.

As Emma began the next verse she opened her eyes. Erin had moved close to her on the left, and Sam came in on the right.

Together, the three of them sang the next verse *a cappella*, in perfect three-part harmony.

> No one could hurt me the way that you do.
> You say that you love me, and I play the fool.
> So why am I crying? And why can't you see
> That no one knows love, especially me?

Now the whole band joined in on their instruments, and the familiar voices of Billy and Pres picked up the next verse with the three girls.

> So if I trust you, show you my heart,
> Will it be the end, or only the start?
> Because no one knows love the way that I do.
> No one knows how to play it so cool.
> So who can I trust? Where should I be?
> No one knows love, especially me.

> No, no one knows love, especially . . .
> me.

Billy, Pres, and the rest of the band dropped out of the song right before the last line, so that only Emma, Sam, and Erin were carrying the tune, *a cappella*. And then Sam and Erin dropped out right before the last word, so that just Emma pronounced the last "me." It brought the song full circle.

When the last note had finally died away, there was silence in the room.

Emma turned to Billy, feeling totally embarrassed. "I told you it wasn't going to be good."

"You're right," Billy said, "it wasn't good."

"I knew it," Emma said, burying her face in her hands.

"It wasn't good," Billy repeated. "It was great. Totally great! It's in the act."

And as if to underline what Billy had said, he, Sam, Erin, Jake, Jay, and Pres all broke into spontaneous, loud applause.

"Are you serious?" Emma cried.

"No, we want to wreck the band by

having you suck," Sam said with a laugh. "Emma, babe, you were fantabulous!"

"Your voice is so pure," Erin agreed. "Really sweet and natural."

"Are you sure?" Emma asked Erin, her face flushed with happiness. "I'm not fishing for compliments. It's just that I don't feel my voice is anywhere near being in your class."

"Well, you can't belt out a blues tune like Erin can," Billy said, "but you can sing stuff she can't sing."

"I'm proud of you, girlfriend," Sam said, giving Emma a hug. "You got yourself a solo!"

"Okay," Billy said, unslinging his guitar, "time for a quick business meeting."

Everyone in the band dutifully filed into the Flirts's living room, which was haphazardly decorated with rock concert posters and a couple of broken-down old convertible couches, and quickly found seats. Billy took his usual place in an old armchair.

"I gotta say, I thought practice went great," Billy said.

"Especially since we haven't rehearsed a

lot lately," Pres observed to Billy with a grin. "No thanks to you, good buddy."

Billy tossed a pillow in Pres's direction. "I'm back now," he said.

"Just make sure you stay back," Jake said.

"This band is the most important thing in my life," Billy said in a low voice.

"I'm telling Carrie you said that!" Sam teased.

Billy leaned over and tugged on Sam's ponytail. "Time to shut up, Samantha."

"Gotcha," Sam agreed. She leaned her head against Pres's shoulder.

"I've got news," Billy said.

"Billy got a call from Polimar Records yesterday," Pres explained. "They're still lookin' closely at us."

Polimar Records! Emma thought. *That's the record company Diana's father bought and then sold. What a nightmare that was—she thought she could control everything. The Flirts were really close to a deal with Polimar, but I thought everything fell through. I guess I was wrong.*

"From Sheldon Call-Me-Shelly Plotkin?"

77

Sam asked good-naturedly. "Get the guy a decent hairpiece!"

Sheldon Plotkin was the artist-and-repertoire executive at Polimar who had first made contact with the band. Not a bad guy, he was a short, chubby, balding, overly enthusiastic man who, Emma now recognized, was just another gear in the big machine of Polimar Records.

"Yup," Billy acknowledged. "It was Shelly."

"He's flying up from New York to take another look at us," Pres explained.

"Later in the summer," Billy continued. "We're gonna do a few club dates around Maine on successive nights."

"This time, the dude said, it's a sure thing," Pres drawled. "I'll believe it when I see it."

"Hey, man," Billy said, "this time it's for real."

"That's fantastic!" Erin cried. "For years I've dreamed about getting a record deal!" She leaned against Jake, whom she was dating on a regular basis.

"Like I said, I'll believe it when I see it,"

Pres repeated. "This dude has strung us along before."

"Ah, but you didn't have me then," Erin teased. "Maybe I'll be your good-luck charm!"

"God knows Diana wasn't," Sam snorted.

Emma remembered how Sam had scoffed when Erin came into the band, because Erin wasn't even close to being thin—she was easily forty pounds overweight—and then how amazed Sam had been that Jake had fallen for her. But Emma knew that Erin was funny, smart, accomplished, and really pretty, in addition to being a size eighteen.

I learned a lot from that, too, Emma recalled, *and now Erin's a really good friend. She's as funny as Sam is . . . well, almost as funny.*

"Anyway, I'll keep you all posted," Billy said. He scratched his chin for a second. "There's something else," he said slowly.

He sounds so serious, Emma thought. *Just like my father did right before he told me he was broke. What could it be?* She leaned forward on the couch.

"It's Sly," Billy explained. "We got a letter from him today."

Sly Smith was the Flirts's original drummer. A slim, totally dedicated guy, Sly had been diagnosed as HIV-positive earlier in the year. Then, a few months later, he'd come down with full-blown AIDS. In fact, Emma knew he'd been hospitalized with *pneumocystis carinii* pneumonia, a common AIDS-related ailment, at Johns Hopkins University Hospital in Baltimore, Maryland, which was where his parents lived.

"He's out of the hospital," Pres said.

"That's good," Erin said. "Isn't it?"

"Just read us the letter," Sam demanded, her voice totally serious for once.

"Okay," Billy said.

Dear Billy,

I'm addressing this letter to you but I want you to read it to all the Flirts, including the girls. I loved the tape you sent me, guys—you sound fabulous. I love the new guy on the drums—what's his name, Jake? Of course, tell him that I could do better.

Everyone laughed.

"Keep reading," Sam urged.

Billy nodded and turned back to the letter.

I'm out of the hospital now, finally. That was a nightmare. I look like hell. I'm sending you a picture with this letter because if I do get to see you guys again, I don't want you to be shocked. Hey, man, when I look in the mirror, *I'm* shocked. I can't believe that this is my life.

The worst thing is that I can't see too well. I've got this virus in my eyes—I can't even pronounce what it's called—and basically it's blinding me, although I can see well enough to write this. The bad news is, I can't watch sports on television. The good news is that you don't have to be able to see to enjoy music.

The doctors tell me that my T-cell count is down around ten, while in healthy people it's over eight hundred. That's not good news. But I'm hanging in there, which is all I can do, and I've got to tell you that every day that I open my eyes—or my ears, as the case may be—is a good day.

I wish I'd learned that a long time ago. I'm here now to tell it to you, so you've got no excuse.

I really miss you guys. Give my best to Sam, Emma, and Carrie, and to the new singer, Erin. And tell them I was wrong—adding backup singers was the best thing that the band ever did.

   Sly

Billy reached into the envelope and pulled out a photograph. Wordlessly he passed it around. Everyone looked at it grimly and passed it on. Finally it came to Emma.

Oh, God, Emma thought, tears coming to her eyes, *he doesn't even look like himself. His hair is so short! And he's so skinny—he looks like he hasn't eaten in months! And there are those lesions on his face.*

"Kinda makes it real, huh?" Billy asked in a low voice.

"I wish there was something we could do," Emma said in a shaky voice, handing the photo back to Billy.

"Oh, there is," Pres replied in his quiet drawl. "Sly added a P.S. to his letter."

"He said," Billy added, "that the best thing we could do for him is to be the best damn rock and roll band in the world."

"Emma?" Jane Hewitt called from the bottom of the stairs. "Phone call for you."

"Thanks, Jane," Emma called back.

Emma had just come upstairs after dinner—pasta with fresh clam sauce made from clams she'd purchased right off one of the boats. She had the evening off, and for once had nothing planned.

Sam's with the twins, Carrie's with her kids, and Kurt's driving his cab tonight, Emma thought as she reached for the phone. *And I'm looking forward to curling up right here with a good book! I only hope it can take my mind off Sly. Compared with Sly's troubles, my father's problems seem almost trivial.*

"Emma Cresswell speaking," Emma said formally.

"Emma! Darling!"

Oh, God, it's my mother. She is the last person I feel like talking to right now.

"Hello, Mother," Emma said. "I haven't talked to you in a long time."

"You could call me anytime you want to, you know," her mother said.

And you could call me, too, Emma thought, *but neither one of us does that very often.*

"So, how are you, Mother?"

"I think it's time my best friend and I had a lovely long chat, don't you?" Kat said gaily.

Emma sighed. "How can we be best friends when we never talk to each other?" she asked her mother in a stiff voice.

"Now, Emma, don't start," Kat said petulantly. "I have a wonderful surprise for you, and you're spoiling it."

"I'm sorry," Emma said quickly, and she really was sorry. *Something about my mother brings out the witch in me,* she realized.

"That's okay, darling," Kat said. "I know just how you can make it up to me."

"How's that, Mother?" Emma asked.

"Come over to see me right this minute for a drink!" Kat cried. "Surprise! I'm on Sunset Island at the Sunset Inn! Now, aren't you thrilled?"

SIX

There she is, Emma thought, spotting her mother sitting by herself at a table on the oceanfront deck of the Sunset Inn. *Looking gorgeous, as always. She may be completely impossible, but she is pretty for a woman in her mid-forties.*

Must be the face-lifts.

Emma, who had been looking forward to an evening of reading, instead had dressed carefully and borrowed the Hewitts' van to meet her mother. She'd chosen a plain white shift made of Egyptian cotton and had slipped white ballet flats on her feet. Unfortunately, as Emma could tell as she approached her mother, Kat had selected something almost exactly the same for herself. The difference was that while Emma's shift was loose and made of cotton, Kat's was fitted and made of raw silk, clearly altered specifically for her contours. With it Kat wore a white straw hat that Emma recognized as a design from the hottest new hat designer in North America.

That hat alone cost her more than Sam's entire wardrobe, Emma thought. *What a waste of money.*

"Why, Emma!" Kat chirped as her daughter approached, "we could be twins! Please do sit down! We'll be like two girlfriends, okay?" Kat leaned over and kissed Emma on both cheeks, as if they were in Europe.

"Fine, Mother," Emma said primly. She hated this part of her mother's personality—the part where Kat refused to act her age. The previous summer, Kat had even been engaged for a while to an artist who was barely older than Emma.

"When did you arrive?" Emma asked. "I mean, this is such a surprise."

"You're not glad to see me?" Kat said in a wounded-little-girl voice.

"It's not that, it's—"

"Then you are glad to see me! Wonderful!" Kat exclaimed.

"It's just a surprise," Emma muttered.

"Life is full of surprises," Kat said obliquely.

Just then one of the tuxedoed waiters set two glasses of chilled champagne down in front of Kat and Emma.

"I ordered for you," Kat said. "I hope champagne agrees with you."

"One glass is all right," Emma replied.

It wasn't too long ago that Emma had been so unhappy that she had drowned her sorrows in wine, night after night. It had never been more than a few glasses at a time, but even that had been too much. It had taken the horrible experience of having a friend die in a drunk-driving accident to shock Emma into never having more than one glass of anything alcoholic.

She picked up the champagne glass with its glistening contents and set it down on a napkin that looked like it was ready to blow away in the night breeze.

"What shall we drink to?" Kat asked, holding up her glass.

Emma gave her mother a querying look.

"A toast," Kat exclaimed. "We must drink a toast. Propose a toast."

To Sly's getting better, Emma thought, *only that's a wish that will never come true. To Dad's getting all his money back, though I don't know if that one will ever come true, either. Well, how about to Kurt and me living happily ever after? But somehow I don't think my mother would appreciate any of those toasts.*

"I can't think of a thing," Emma told her mother.

"Well," Kat said, a little huffily, "I'll propose one, then: To surprises."

Emma lifted her glass. "To surprises," she agreed stiffly.

Kat took a dainty sip. "Lovely," she commented. "Like the lovely surprise your father had this week."

"It wasn't lovely," Emma began, "it was—"

"Emma, it's called irony." Kat interrupted her daughter. "I am being ironic."

"Oh." Emma stared at the table.

"Well," Kat said, "your father was poor

when I first met him. He'll just have to pick up the pieces."

"You could help him," Emma said quickly.

"I should think not," Kat replied, taking another sip of champagne. "Not after this week of foolishness. Bankruptcy, indeed. How utterly humiliating!"

"It's not his fault!" Emma protested.

"It most certainly is," Kat replied. "Just ask him; he'll tell you. Brent Cresswell, bankrupt. It is all over the Boston papers."

"Well," Emma said, squeezing the stem of her champagne glass in anger, "I bet a lot of other people lost money this week."

"Observant of you," Kat commented dryly. "But none of the others is named Cresswell. Do you have any idea of the way people are talking?"

"I don't care," Emma said.

"Well, you should," Kat said. "You're a Cresswell, too. He's dragging your name through the mud."

"Oh, Mother, that's a ridiculous way to look at things—"

"Don't lecture me, Emma," her mother said sharply. "You are talking about things you know nothing about." Kat drank from her glass again, then set it down. "I, on the other hand, made money."

Emma was shocked. The financial markets of the world had plummeted all week, and her mother had actually *made* money? How was this possible?

"Don't look so surprised, Emma," Kat said smugly. "It's true."

"What did you do?" Emma asked.

"I anticipated the market's fall," Kat explained, as if she were a college professor explaining the simplest thing in the world to a somewhat slow student. "So I told our financial manager to liquidate the family securities portfolio a month ago."

"What did that do?"

"That," Kat said triumphantly, "put us in all-cash positions. He thought I was crazy then, but he's worshiping at my feet now. Then, just for fun, I had him buy certain stock options that allowed me to . . . well, let's just say we're in a better position now than we were before this week began."

"How much better?" Emma queried.

"Oh, about thirty million dollars better,"

Kat said nonchalantly, taking another sip of champagne and rolling it around in her mouth with her tongue.

"Thirty million dollars?" Emma repeated.

"Give or take a million or so," Kat said. "Honestly, perhaps I should demand that Brent give me his job!" Kat laughed at her own joke.

"That's amazing," Emma said in admiration. She'd had no idea that her mother had the slightest knowledge of anything financial at all.

"Well, it's just money," Kat said carelessly. "When you've had it in the family long enough, you get used to making it, sort of like coffee in the morning!" Kat smiled brightly.

"Well, I admit," Emma said, "I'm impressed."

"Thank you, dear," Kat said. "Anyway, I came up to tell you myself, so you shouldn't worry."

"I wasn't worrying," Emma told her mother, reaching to nibble on one of the cashew nuts that were in a glass dish on the table.

"Good," Kat said. "It's so . . . *common* to worry about money, don't you think?"

"A lot of people don't have any choice," Emma pointed out.

"Oh, well, little people, I suppose," Kat agreed dismissively.

"Not little people," Emma said. "It's just luck that you were born rich!"

"And you, too, my darling," Kat said. "I don't think you'd know how to live without it!" She eyed her daughter carefully.

Something is going on in her mind, Emma thought. *I've seen that conniving look on her face before, and it's never led to anything good. . . .*

"So," Kat said brightly, "let's talk of things more interesting than money. You'll have to tell me everything that's going on with you. Did I tell you I had my hair done at Chez Louis again last week?"

Kat prattled on, and Emma listened. As usual, most of the conversation revolved completely around her mother's life, her friends, and her social events.

They never quite got around to Emma's social life. Kat never asked about Kurt

Ackerman, and Emma avoided bringing it up herself.

Good thing, too, Emma thought as the evening wore on. *Because I don't think Kat is going to be too excited that Kurt and I are an item again.*

"You didn't tell your mother about Kurt?" Sam exclaimed into the phone.

"No," Emma admitted quietly, shifting the telephone from her left shoulder to her right.

"Good," Sam said.

"Good?" Emma echoed.

"Of course it's good."

"Why?" Emma asked, totally perplexed.

"Because as soon as you tell her," Sam pronounced, "she's going to kill you."

It was the next morning. Emma was taking care of Katie and Wills Hewitt, while Sam was home alone giving herself a manicure, since both Becky and Allie Jacobs were off at Club Sunset Island, where they were counselors-in-training.

The weather had turned miserable again. But instead of a single, long, drenching rain, there seemed to be waves of thunderstorms rolling across the island.

At least the septic tank at the country club hasn't gone out again, Emma thought. That's something to be grateful for!

Emma had called Sam just to chat, and to fill her in on Kat's surprise visit. Since Katie Hewitt was upstairs in her mother's room watching MTV again and Wills was engrossed in a book, this had seemed like a good time.

"I don't have to wait for my mother to kill me," Emma replied. "Jane Hewitt's going to take care of that for her, I'm sure."

"How come?" Sam asked.

"Katie exceeded her daily TV quota about an hour ago," Emma explained.

"She's watching MTV again?"

"You guessed it," Emma said.

"Carrie says Chloe is doing the same thing," Sam said.

"She's into MTV?" Emma queried.

"Black Entertainment Network," Sam replied. "She hates everything except rap now."

"Katie's into rap," Emma said. "But also rock and roll and metal."

"Well, you can't fault her taste in music," Sam joked. "At least it isn't country."

"Pres likes country," Emma said.

"It's some southern genetic thing," Sam quipped. "Anyway, you're going to have to tell good ol' Mom about Kurt, aren't you?"

"Why?" Emma asked. "Give me one good reason."

"Because she's your mother," Sam said.

"Sam, we're talking about Kat Cresswell here. She's not a normal mother."

"True," Sam allowed. "You're right. Your mother is a major piece of work. Keep everything important from her for as long as possible, because she'll only try to use it against you."

Emma shifted the phone back to her other shoulder. "Just a sec," she said to Sam, and then stuck her hand over the receiver. The music from the TV was getting too overbearing.

"Hey!" Emma yelled up the stairs to Katie. "Turn it down a little!" Incredibly, Katie did actually lower the volume on the TV.

"Sorry," she said to Sam. "MTV drown-out."

"I understand," Sam replied. "Anyway, Kat would totally flip out about Kurt, right?"

"That's an understatement," Emma said dryly. "My mother thought I was crazy to want to marry Kurt. When she finds out we're together again . . ."

"So she won't find out," Sam said.

"But she's here on the island!" Emma cried. "What am I supposed to do, sneak around behind her back like I'm thirteen years old?"

"Exactly," Sam said. "Take a page out of the twins' book. That's exactly what they would do."

"But I'm nineteen years old!" Emma exclaimed. "It seems ridiculous!"

"Here's my advice, O Ice Princess," Sam intoned.

"Tell me," Emma encouraged her.

"Play it super cool with Aquaman until your mother leaves. And keep your mouth absolutely shut. When's she leaving?"

"That's the problem," Emma said. "I don't know."

"Well, she never stays very long," Sam pointed out. "After all, she isn't the center of attention here."

"True," Emma agreed.

"So it can't be for more than a few days at the most," Sam continued. "Just kind of stay away from Kurt for a few days, and then Kat will split and you and Kurt can make up for lost time!"

"I don't know," Emma said doubtfully. "Maybe you were right in the first place. I should just tell her and deal with the consequences. . . ."

"I don't think so," Sam said firmly. "Because she *will* go ballistic. One of your parents already has had a heart attack, and I'm getting tired of taking the ferry to the Maine Medical Center."

Emma laughed and sat down on one of the kitchen chairs.

"Besides," Sam added, "the food in the cafeteria there sucks."

Emma laughed again. "You should be a psychologist," she said.

"I don't think so," Sam replied. "I can't stand dealing with other people's problems."

"What are you doing tonight?" Emma asked, changing the subject.

"Pres and I are going to the movies in Portland," she answered. "Wanna come?"

"No," Emma replied pensively. "I'm sure my mother is going to want to have dinner with me."

"Come afterward," Sam urged. "We're seeing some French movie Pres heard about."

"You hate movies with subtitles."

"Not when Pres is sitting next to me, I don't," Sam said. "Dark theater, nobody there but us, intertwined hands, steamy love scenes on the screen . . . whoa, baby!"

Emma laughed again. "It sounds like fun. But I told Kurt we could get together after nine. He's driving the cab until then."

"You think that's safe?" Sam asked.

"Come on. I'm not even going to meet him until really late."

"Have you told him yet? That your mother is here on his precious island?" Sam wanted to know. "Or aren't you going to tell him about her, either?"

"I don't know," Emma said with a sigh. "I haven't said anything yet."

"He'll be overcome with joy," Sam said sarcastically.

"That's what I thought," Emma agreed.

"Anyway," Sam concluded, "remember the Bridges advice. Keep her from him and him from her and everything will be just ducky."

"Agreed," Emma said. "And one thing above all: never, never, never invite both of them to dinner at the same time!"

"Not unless you invite Kurt's dad, too!" Sam teased before she said good-bye and hung up.

Could you imagine a dinner with Kat, me, Kurt, and Kurt's dad together? Emma thought with a shudder as she hung up the phone. *Everyone would hate everyone. And I would be served as dessert!*

SEVEN

"It's a gorgeous night," Emma murmured in Kurt's ear as the two of them cuddled together on a blanket up against the dunes.

"If we stay dry," Kurt whispered back, grinning happily. "We've got to be slightly crazy to be out here now."

Crazy in love, Emma thought, breathing in the humid night air.

"Definitely out of our minds is more like it," Kurt amended thoughtfully as flashes of heat lightning lit up the evening sky and illuminated the beach. There was no one on the main beach besides the two of them.

"It's only heat lightning," Emma said. "It's really far away."

"Where did you learn about heat lightning?" Kurt teased good-naturedly.

"Katie Hewitt," Emma responded with a smile. "She's obsessed with two things—MTV and the Weather Channel."

Kurt laughed. "She's such a great kid. I'd love to have a daughter like her someday."

Emma turned to look at him. "Not someday soon, I hope."

"No, Ms. Cresswell," Kurt teased, tickling her in the ribs. "Not soon. Someday in the far-off future."

I want kids, too, Emma mused. *A little girl. And I'll make her feel so much more loved than I ever felt. . . .*

"You're lost in thought," Kurt observed, pulling Emma close.

"I was just thinking about the future," Emma murmured.

"It'll take care of itself," Kurt said easily. "That's my new motto."

Wow, he really has changed, she thought. *No more pushing me to make commitments that I'm not ready to make.*

"You're terrific," she said impetuously, giving him a loud smack on the cheek.

"Gee, thanks," Kurt replied, grinning at her. "You're not so bad yourself."

Emma smiled and watched the sky light up again. *What could have been a depressing evening tonight has turned out great. I had dinner with Kat at the inn, and it wasn't even that excruciating. Then she said she felt tired and went in early to bed, so it was easy for me to meet up with Kurt after he was done driving the cab. And what could be more romantic than a night on a deserted beach with the guy I think is the greatest?*

Of course, I haven't told him that my mother is here on the island. Or that I didn't tell her that he and I are seeing each other again . . .

She felt a pang of guilt, even though the advice Sam had given her that afternoon—to keep her mouth shut no matter what—had seemed at the time to be the right thing to do.

Now it just seems ridiculously immature, Emma realized. *If I want Kurt to be totally honest with me, then I have to be totally honest with him.*

"Hey, major lightning!" Kurt said, pointing to a streak in the sky. He turned to her. "Major electric kisses," he added, and kissed her until she felt breathless.

"Mmm, I love that," Emma whispered against Kurt's neck.

"Then I should probably keep doing it," Kurt replied, lightly brushing his lips against Emma's cheek, her jawline, and then her neck.

I need to tell him about my mother. As much as she loved Kurt's kisses, the thought kept nagging at her brain. *So what if he doesn't like her? Not that I can blame him. But she's always going to be my mother.*

"Kurt?" Emma said softly, sitting up a little.

"Hmm?" he murmured, nuzzling her neck.

"I've got something to tell you," Emma said.

"Is it important?" Kurt asked.

"Kind of," Emma replied softly.

"If it's not really important," Kurt joked,

kissing Emma lightly on the ear, "save it. Because right now I'm in heaven and am not to be disturbed."

"Well, we decided we need to be really open with each other," Emma reminded him.

"Right, so tell me later."

"I just wanted to let you know that my mother is making one of her surprise visits to Sunset Island," Emma said very quickly.

Emma felt Kurt stiffen for a moment, then relax.

"Well, I can't really tell her not to come visit her daughter," Kurt said philosophically.

"That's true," Emma replied, pleased that Kurt was taking it so well.

"And I can't call out the National Guard. When is she coming?" he asked lightly.

"Uh . . . she did. I mean, she's here on the island now."

"Well, that means I don't have to worry about when she's showing up, then, do I?" Kurt said with a chuckle.

"You're taking this really well," Emma marveled.

"Em, she's your mother. There's nothing either of us can do about that."

"True," Emma agreed.

"So where's she staying? With the Popes?" Kurt asked. The Popes were very wealthy friends of Emma's mother who had a summer house on the island.

"Sunset Inn," Emma replied. Off in the distance, some thunder from another of the storms that had been rolling across the island all day boomed slightly, like someone hitting a bass drum.

"So?" Kurt said, folding his arms and leaning back against the dune. "Fill me in. Why is she here?"

Emma sighed. "That's just it. I don't know. It's very strange."

"She didn't tell you why she came?"

Emma shook her head. "And you know my mother. She always has some kind of plan. She's never come to see me just to see me." Emma reached for a handful of sand and let it trickle between her fingers. "She did report that whereas my dad lost all his money in the stock-market crash, she made a bundle."

"What's a bundle?" Kurt asked.

"Thirty million or so."

Kurt was speechless for a moment. "I don't think I'll ever get used to those kind of numbers," he finally said. "All I think about is how many hungry kids could be fed with that money, or how many houses built for the homeless . . . but I have a feeling that's not what she's going to do with the money."

"I can't control my mother," Emma pointed out.

"No, you can't," Kurt agreed. He put his arm around her. "So, you don't think she hopped over to the island just to tell you about her new millions on top of her old millions, huh?"

"No," Emma said thoughtfully, leaning back against Kurt's arm. "I can't quite put my finger on it, but I know her too well. Something is up."

"She'll tell you eventually," Kurt said. "Meanwhile, what did she say about us?"

"Us?" Emma echoed nervously.

"About our being together again," Kurt said. "She was only the happiest woman on the face of the earth when we broke up."

Emma was silent for a second. And then she knew she had to tell Kurt the truth.

"I haven't actually said anything to her," she managed. "About you and me."

"You haven't said a word?" Kurt asked incredulously, looking at Emma with his piercing blue eyes.

"It didn't come up," Emma said defensively.

"How is that possible?" Kurt answered.

"You know my mother," Emma replied as another roll of thunder sounded off in the distance. "She never talks about anything but herself."

"You're allowed to change the subject, you know," Kurt said.

"It's been a constant Kat monologue," Emma reported truthfully. *Of course, it's true I never interrupted it to tell her about him, either,* she thought honestly.

"I don't owe her anything, anyway," Emma went on, kicking at the sand near their blanket. "It's none of her business that I'm seeing you."

"Wait a sec," Kurt said. "That's not fair."

"What's not fair about it?"

"I get into a giant hassle almost every

day with my father about you, but somehow you don't have to tell your mother?"

"I'm not living in my mother's house," Emma said defensively. "It's not the same thing."

"So you and I play by different rules because I live with my parent and you don't?"

"No, that's not it, but—"

"But what?" Kurt demanded. "I don't get it."

Silence.

"Look," Emma finally said, "you're going to the Air Force Academy in the fall, and I'm going back to Goucher."

"True," Kurt said.

"And you're the one who told me we should take it one day at a time," Emma reminded him.

"That doesn't mean we shouldn't be honest, for pete's sake!" Kurt exclaimed.

"I just don't want to deal with her about this, Kurt!"

"Because she's so difficult."

"Exactly!" Emma agreed.

"My father isn't exactly a piece of cake, you know," Kurt reminded her. He stared at her for a moment. "I still feel it's because you're ashamed of me—"

"Never!" Emma cried. "I love you!"

"—and you're afraid that she'll be mad at you because we're together again," Kurt continued. "After what happened."

Emma took Kurt's face in her hands. "Kurt, I could never, ever be ashamed of you. I love you. You must know that."

"But she hates me," Kurt stated matter-of-factly against a background of faint thunder.

"And your father hates me," Emma said softly.

"And my father knows we're together," Kurt said pointedly.

Emma sat back and sighed. "I'm sorry. This visit completely took me by surprise. I just don't want to go through what she'd probably put me through. Especially when we don't know what's going to happen in the fall."

"We don't?" Kurt asked.

"I mean, we'll be in two different places," Emma said, looking at him carefully.

"Right," Kurt agreed.

Please tell me that you'll still love me

even if we're far from each other, Emma wanted to beg. *Please tell me this isn't going to end!*

"Look, I'm not saying I think you're right," Kurt said slowly, "but I do see how you feel. You don't have to tell her. I can deal with it."

"Are you sure?"

"No," Kurt admitted. "I keep feeling that you want it both ways, Em. You want us to have some commitment past this summer, but you don't want to deal with the reaction that you would get from your mom."

"I just don't want to complicate things," Emma said.

"Okay," Kurt agreed. "It's your call." He pulled her to him for a kiss.

In Emma's heart, she knew Kurt was right. *I want it both ways,* she realized. *A commitment and no commitment at the same time.*

Either way I'm going to lose.

"It's midnight," Kurt whispered, looking at his luminous watch. "We'd better go."

Emma sat up and rubbed her eyes. "We fell asleep?" she asked.

"We fell asleep," Kurt confirmed, caressing Emma's cheek.

"We're still dry," Emma whispered.

"It's clearing up now," Kurt explained. As if to underscore his point, a fresh breeze swept along the beach, blowing tiny grains of sand into their faces.

"What a nap!" Emma said. "Delicious!"

"I agree," Kurt said. He got to his feet, reached down for Emma, and helped pull her to her feet. Then he turned her around and patted the back of her T-shirt and jeans, brushing off the sand.

After Emma had done the same for him, Kurt gathered up their blanket in his left arm and put his right arm around Emma, and the two of them started back to the main parking lot on the far side of the Sunset Inn. Emma slipped her arm around Kurt, and they walked silently arm in arm by the water's edge, the fresh westerly breeze blowing crazily at their hair.

They walked for ten minutes, past the boardwalk, past the Sunset Inn, until they were finally at the parking lot. Then Emma heard a familiar voice behind her, and her heart sank down into her feet.

"Emma, oh Emma!"

Emma and Kurt turned around. Kurt gave Emma's hand a little squeeze, but Emma couldn't make her hand move in response.

It was Kat Cresswell, not fifty feet behind them, dressed in a jet-black designer jogging outfit, running shoes on her feet.

She must have had insomnia, Emma thought, her heart sinking, *and she decided to go for a walk. Great timing. Just perfect.*

"The best-laid plans of mice and men," Kurt said lightly, holding on to Emma's hand. "I learned that one in a course on Shakespeare."

"Meaning we're about to get busted," Emma said back.

"You got it," Kurt agreed.

Emma and Kurt stood silently, holding hands, as Kat approached. Oddly, Kat was smiling. But Emma recognized the smile.

It's the same smile she had when we gave that rehearsal dinner at Rubie's Diner, Emma recalled. *She's smiling, but she looks like she could spit nails. That's the smile of a snake about to strike!*

"Hello, Mother," Emma forced herself to say. "What a coincidence."

"Hello, darling," Kat said, her smile still in place.

"Hello, Mrs. Cresswell," Kurt said politely.

"Oh, you know you should call me Kat," Emma's mother said.

"Kat," Kurt said evenly.

"Well, how interesting to run into the two of you. Together," Kat added, carefully pushing her hair off her face.

"I was going to tell you," Emma began guiltily.

"We decided together not to tell you," Kurt said. "We thought you'd make it uncomfortable for Emma."

"Well, how very gallant of you!" Kat exclaimed. "That's a very noble quality, Kurt." Somehow Emma knew she didn't mean it as a compliment.

"Not particularly," Kurt said. "It was probably very self-serving."

"Hmm, perhaps," Kat agreed.

Why isn't she acting more shocked? Emma wondered. *Or is she that good an actress?*

"Emma, darling," Kat continued, "do arrange to meet me for lunch tomorrow, say one-ish, at the club."

"I don't know if I can get off work, Mother," Emma said stiffly.

"Oh, I'm sure you'll find a way. It's terribly important."

"Look, Mrs. Cresswell, if you have something to say about Emma and me being together, why don't you just say it now and save us all a lot of time?" Kurt suggested. "I know this is a shock to you. . . ."

Kat laughed a high, girlish laugh. "A shock? You're such a silly boy. No, dear, this isn't a shock."

"It isn't?" Emma asked incredulously.

"Hardly," Kat said. "My dear friend Mrs. Pope called me, very concerned, to tell me that she'd seen you together everywhere. Obviously the two of you are an item once again."

"She did?" Emma managed.

"She did." Kat smiled her icy grin again. "Why do you think I'm here, Emma?"

"You could have just called and asked me," Emma said, heat coming to her face.

"But it's patently obvious you would have lied to me," Kat said.

"It's probably all for the best that it's out in the open," Kurt said. "Look, I—"

"Excuse me, Kurt," Kat said, cutting him off. She turned to her daughter. "Tomorrow. One o'clock, dear. Your future depends on it."

EIGHT

"Cheer up, Emma," Sam said.

"Why?" Emma asked, rubbing her forehead wearily. "What's to cheer up about?"

"It could be worse." Sam unwrapped a piece of bubble gum and popped it into her mouth.

It was shortly before one the next afternoon, and Sam and Emma were at the country club, dangling their feet in the pool.

"How?" Emma asked, slapping the water with the ball of one foot.

"Kurt could be coming to lunch with you and your mother," Sam quipped.

"You're right, that would be worse," Emma

agreed. She jerked back to avoid the splash from some kid who'd just done a cannonball dive off the high board.

"Or you could have been wearing his engagement ring again when she saw you," Sam said mischievously, reaching over and splashing Emma.

Emma managed a smile. "She probably would have had me kidnapped by one of those cult deprogrammers."

"If you disappear suddenly, that's the first thing I'll think of," Sam promised.

Emma looked at her watch and sighed. "Well, time for me to go in and face Kat."

"If you need help, call 911 and tell them you're in labor," Sam suggested.

"You could make me laugh at a funeral," Emma commented gratefully.

"I hope so, because it seems to me you're about to go to your own!" Sam joked.

Emma got up slowly, pulled a pair of white cotton pants and a cropped embroidered white cotton shirt over her pale pink bathing suit, slipped into a pair of sandals, and turned slowly toward the main building, which housed the country club dining room.

"If you walked any slower," Sam called to Emma as she trudged unenthusiastically toward the dining room, "you'd be going backward!"

Emma turned, gave her friend a helpless shrug, and continued into the dining room. She spotted her mother immediately and walked over to her table for two in a quiet corner of the dining room.

"Hello, darling," Kat said. "Don't you have some lovely color."

"I was out by the pool," Emma said tonelessly.

"And I see you didn't bother to dress for lunch," Kat noted. She shook her head sadly. "You never used to go around like that."

Emma noticed her mother had on a perfect summer pants suit by a well-known French designer. Her straw hat matched the subtlest tone in the jacket's fabric, as did her shoes.

"Like what?" Emma asked sharply.

"Unkempt, dear," Kat said, wiping moisture off the outside of her wine glass.

I will not let her get to me, Emma vowed. She reached for the glass of water that had just been poured by the ever-attentive waiter and took a sip.

"I've ordered two chef's salads," Kat declared, not even asking if Emma wanted anything else, "so we don't need menus."

"Fine," Emma said. *I couldn't eat a bite, anyway.*

"So, what do you have to say for yourself?" Kat asked, as if they were two friends having a casual lunch.

What can I possibly say? she wondered. *Anything I say is going to be wrong, so why should I bother to say anything at all? In fact, why am I even here? I should just get up and leave. But I can't!*

And then Emma remembered some advice she'd been given by the psychotherapist she had seen after her first split-up with Kurt.

"People may think they have the right to say all kinds of things to you about your relationship with Kurt," Mrs. Miller had said. "That doesn't mean you have to respond to them."

Great, Emma thought sourly. *Does that also apply to my mother?*

"Emma," Kat finally said with a sigh, "I

have to tell you, I am disappointed in you. *Severely* disappointed in you."

"Why didn't you just tell me when you first arrived why you were here?" Emma asked. "Why did you play such a silly game?"

Kat smiled. "You are hardly one to be talking about games right now, young lady." She tasted her wine and made a face. "House wine. You'd think they could do better." She put her glass down. "I want you to know I've tried to think calmly about all of this, though I can assure you it hasn't been easy."

"I imagine not," Emma said stiffly, wishing she could be anywhere else besides where she was at that moment—even out on a double date with Diana De Witt!

Her mother was silent for a long moment.

"How could you?" Kat finally cried, all pretense behind her. "How could you do this to us?"

"To *us*?" Emma responded, trying to keep her voice low. "I didn't do anything to *us*."

"How can you be so totally self-centered?" Kat went on, ignoring Emma's response.

"*Me?*" Emma practically screamed. "You're the one who—"

"Keep your voice down, Emma, you're making a scene," Kat hissed.

Emma took a large gulp of air. "Mother, you are the most self-centered person I've ever met," she said in a low voice.

Kat shook her head. "You love to hurt me. You always have. It gives you some kind of perverse joy, I suppose. I will never understand why."

They fell silent while the waiter brought over their salads and refilled their water glasses.

"Mother," Emma said after a minute, trying hard to control herself, "I am not cruel and I don't enjoy hurting you—or anyone else, for that matter."

Kat gave a short, bitter laugh. "You know, it amazes me. Your father and you do your very best to ruin your lives and then you expect me to understand, to act as if it isn't a reflection on me and the entire family."

That's not fair, Emma thought. *It's almost as if she thinks I chose Kurt—and Daddy lost money in the stock-market crash—just to make her suffer! Not to mention that she thinks I'm ruining my life by being with Kurt.*

"Whatever you say," Emma said tersely. She picked up her fork and jabbed it into a lettuce leaf.

Kat leaned forward. "Emma, all I've ever wanted is to be your friend. But you persist in pushing me away."

"You don't act like a friend," Emma replied.

"Because you won't allow me to be one," Kat said, sitting back. "I'm going to ask you this calmly, and I'm going to try to understand your point of view. What on earth do you see in that, that . . . that cab driver?"

"He's—"

"He's a low-class cab driver!"

"That's totally unfair and you know it," Emma spat out. "He's a college student, and he drives a taxi to put himself through school."

"People are defined by what they do," Kat said firmly. "You dropped this boy once—more than once, as I recall. After you almost married him, and then didn't, I thought we had dodged an enormous bullet."

"I wasn't ready to get married," Emma responded quietly.

"Well, your immaturity is readily apparent, so I'll have to agree with you on that score," Kat said.

"Isn't it nice that we can agree on something," Emma replied icily. *Oh, my God,* she realized, *I sound just like my mother! I don't ever want to turn into her!*

Kat took a small bite of her salad, then put her fork down. "Do you just want the chance to drop him again?"

"Of course not," Emma replied, a lump rising in her throat.

Kat took a sip of her wine. "I only want to look at it logically," she said.

"Fine," Emma snapped.

"One, he comes from a lower-class family—"

"Yes, but—"

"Don't interrupt me. Two, his family is not only poor, they're not educated."

Emma nodded weakly. What could she say?

"Three," Kat continued, "his father detests you—you told me so after the almost-wedding."

"His father—"

"Four," Kat continued, "he drives a taxicab for a living, and five, you had the good sense to drop him before." Kat gave Emma a cool, knowing look. "Really, Emma, no man is so good in bed as to be worth ruining your life!"

Emma felt her face burning with rage and humiliation. "For your information, Mother—not that it's any of your business—Kurt and I haven't slept together."

"You don't expect me to believe that," Kat said coldly.

"You can believe whatever you like—you always do—but I happen to be telling you the truth."

"Since you lie so often, how could I possibly tell?" Kat asked.

Emma threw her hands in the air. "I give up!"

Kat reached over and touched Emma's arm. "You think I don't understand what it's like to be in lust, dear, but I do."

"I don't want to have this conversation!"

Emma yelled. "You don't hear a word I'm saying!"

"My point, which you so childishly choose to ignore," Kat said in a low voice, "is that you can lust after a rich boy as easily as you can lust after a poor boy. What about Trent Hayden-Bishop?"

Emma shuddered. Trent Hayden-Bishop was a guy from Boston, a year older than her. She and Trent had grown up together; Kat and Trent's parents were constantly trying to fix them up. They were a perfect match: the same education, lots of family money, lots of common interests, the same background.

There was only one problem. Emma loathed him.

I had a dream a while ago in which I was actually married to Trent, Emma recalled. *And it was one of the worst nightmares of my life!*

"I don't think that's a very good idea," Emma managed. She stared at her mother. "I love Kurt. It might be difficult for you to understand—"

"Emma, you don't even know what love is," Kat said sadly.

"Oh, and you do?" Emma shot back, immediately getting angry all over again. She held up her hand. "Mother, I don't want to continue this. It's ridiculous. I love Kurt. We've both made mistakes, but now we're together again. We've changed."

"So," Kat said in a businesslike fashion. "You are going to continue to see this taxicab driver?"

"Yes," Emma said.

"You are going to marry him, and then he's going to live off your money?"

"Wrong, Mother," Emma said triumphantly. "Kurt would like it much better if I were poor. He's as far from a gold-digger as anyone you ever met."

"Really?" Kat marveled. "How lovely for you." She toyed with the stem of her wineglass. "You must know that there are always consequences for your actions—or choices, in this case."

"Of course," Emma said, but wondered what her mother was talking about.

"I am asking you once more not to see him," Kat requested.

"I won't do that," Emma said.

"Very well," Kat noted. "Please remember that this is your decision."

"It is." Emma nodded. "I'm sorry that you disagree with it so much, because it—"

Kat looked at her watch. "Lunch is over," she said, pushing her chair away from the table, her salad essentially uneaten. She stood up. "I have to call George Bledsoe."

Emma was puzzled, and then she blanched. *George Bledsoe?* she thought. *He's our family's lawyer. What's she going to do? Oh, God, is she going to get a restraining order to prevent Kurt from seeing me? No!*

"You can't do that," Emma said angrily. "No court would give you a restraining order against Kurt. I'm over eighteen and—"

Kat laughed. And then laughed some more. And then sat down again. "Oh, Emma," she said with mirth, "is that what you think I'm going to do?"

"I wouldn't put it past you to try," Emma said. "But it won't work."

"I wouldn't do that," Kat said. "You may see whomever you want."

Emma was incredulous. *I stuck up for*

myself, and it worked! she thought triumphantly.

"Thank you, Mother," she said gratefully. "I want you to know how much I appreciate that."

"I am calling George Bledsoe," Kat went on, "to talk about your trusts. And my will."

Suddenly it dawned on Emma exactly what her mother was talking about—Emma's inheritance.

"All it will take is one phone call," Kat said, "and all the trusts will be changed, plus my will, and you will learn once and for all exactly what the consequences are of turning your back on your family."

I'd be poor, Emma realized. She sat there, dumbfounded. "I can't believe you'd do that to me," she finally said.

"Didn't you just tell me Kurt would prefer you poor?" Kat reminded Emma smugly.

"I just can't believe—"

"Emma, I'm doing this for your own good!" Kat exclaimed.

"I doubt that very much," Emma said quietly.

Kat drummed her French-manicured nails on the table. "All right," she said. "Perhaps I'm moving too quickly. Perhaps I should give you some time to think about this. I'm going to wait, oh, let's say another two days before I call George. It's perfectly pleasant on this island. I'm sure I can entertain myself."

Emma couldn't muster any words.

"Then," Kat continued, "if you tell me that you're never going to see the taxi driver again, we can forget this entire conversation. Okay?"

Emma just stared at her mother.

"Good," Kat said, as if Emma had agreed with her. "Think it over carefully. And we can talk again the day after tomorrow. Just like the two best friends we are."

NINE

"That is the most incredible story I've ever heard," Carrie said after she heard Emma's version of her lunch with her mother.

"It's the truth," Emma said.

It was the next afternoon, and Emma and Sam were over at the Templetons' house, hanging out in the kitchen.

The crashing and banging of Ian Templeton's band, Lord Whitehead and the Zit People, which was rehearsing at that very moment in the basement, carried up into the kitchen. The rehearsal was why all the girls were over at Carrie's employer's house. Since Katie was on a special play date,

Emma had brought Ethan and Wills Hewitt to check out the rehearsal.

"I can't believe she'd really do it—cut you off without a penny," Sam said.

"I don't know if she'd really do it or not," Emma admitted. "She might."

"Your mother is amazing," Sam said. "Just when you think you've got her figured out— Just a sec."

Sam got up and walked into the hallway and slammed the door to the basement shut. "I truly cannot listen to that crap and think at the same time."

"They won't even notice," Carrie said. "They're even more into it than usual."

Ian's band played "industrial music," which apparently was something that Ian had invented. Industrial music consisted of the members of the band banging iron and wooden rods on the insides of hulked-out household appliances while a tape of some popular rock song played in the background. Sometimes Ian recited romantic poetry by Keats and Lord Byron to the accompaniment of the loud banging.

Emma looked at her watch. "I have to be back at the Hewitts' in forty-five minutes," she said. "I feel like I'm walking around in a daze."

"You're planning to talk to Jane about this, right?" Carrie asked.

"Yes, or Jeff," Emma said, nibbling thoughtfully on a stalk of celery that Carrie had put out as a snack. "I have no idea what the legal basis of all of this is."

"I just cannot imagine . . ." Sam mused.

"What?" Emma asked.

"You. Poor. You wouldn't be you anymore!" Sam exclaimed.

"I'd be exactly the same," Emma said defensively.

"No offense, Em," Sam said, "but only someone who has always been rich would think that."

"Hey, be nice," Carrie warned Sam playfully. "Emma is stressed."

"I know," Sam agreed. She turned to Emma. "And I promise to love you, rich or poor . . . but it sure would be weird! No more doing whatever you want whenever you want, no more designer clothes—"

"Let's focus here," Carrie cut in. "We have to try to help Emma out. Have you told Kurt yet?"

"No," Emma admitted, reaching for a carrot stick. She dipped it in the French onion dip and crunched it in her mouth. "I can't."

"He loves you; he won't care," Carrie said.

"Your money was always a problem for him," Sam pointed out.

Emma took a slice of cucumber and popped it in her mouth. "I meant I haven't had a chance to tell him. He's driving until nine tonight."

"So you'll tell him then?" Carrie pressed.

"I guess," Emma said with a sigh. "Though what I'm going to say, I don't know." She reached into the bowl of potato chips and grabbed a handful.

"Just tell him the truth," Carrie said.

"Bad advice," Sam stated. "I say the best defense is a good offense."

"With Kurt?" Emma asked in confusion.

"No!" Sam replied quickly. "With your mother. Go on the offensive."

"What are you talking about?" She stretched out her hand for more chips.

"Whoa, you *are* majorly stressed, girlfriend. You are chowing down kind of like me," Sam told Emma. "You wouldn't want to end up poor *and* fat!"

"Just explain what you meant," Emma demanded.

"Okay, it's like this," Sam said. "Lie."

"Lie?" Carrie echoed dubiously.

"Exactly," Sam confirmed. She turned to Emma. "Go to Kat, tell her she's right, she wins, fine, cool, you're not going to see Kurt again."

"That's terrible advice!" Carrie exclaimed.

"I could never do that," Emma said. "It's not fair to Kurt."

"Give me a break!" Sam cried. "Is what your mother's trying to do to you fair?"

"No," Emma started, "but—"

"No buts about it," Sam stated. "If you try to do what's right with someone who's not playing by the rules, you'll lose every time."

"But—"

"Okay, say you're playing Monopoly, and someone steals lots of money from the bank," Sam expounded. "Unless you steal money, too, you'll always lose the game."

"How about confronting the person who's

stealing the money?" Carrie asked with an arched eyebrow.

"They'll just deny it," Sam said with a shrug. "It's human nature!"

"You don't think much of your fellow humans, do you?" Carrie said.

"Carrie, the whole world doesn't march for world peace like your family does," Sam pointed out. "Your average human on the street is basically a scumbag."

"Sam!" Carrie exclaimed. "I know you don't believe that!"

"Can we get back to my mother, please?" Emma asked.

"Sorry," Carrie said. She folded her arms and leaned thoughtfully against the kitchen counter. "Let's look at this ruthlessly for a moment."

"Let's," Sam agreed.

"Emma couldn't get away with lying to Kat, even if she wanted to."

"That's true," Emma agreed. "I'm sure she'd have the Popes on her payroll as spies."

"Nah, the Popes are too rich," Sam said. "Knowing Kat, she'd just hire a private detective to follow you."

"I wouldn't put it past her," Emma said sadly.

"I suppose you and Kurt could stop seeing each other for a while. . . ." Carrie said slowly.

"You know Kurt would never agree to that," Emma said. She nervously reached for more potato chips, and then stopped herself.

"I can't believe she thinks she has the right to tell me who I can love!" Emma said bitterly. "This is the lowest thing she's ever done."

"Mondo controlling," Sam agreed. "It's like a sick game show. Behind door number one, the cute guy! Behind door number two, twenty million dollars!"

If Sam only knew how much money was really involved . . . Emma thought humorlessly.

"Guys come and go," Sam quipped, "but twenty million dollars is twenty million dollars."

Emma looked at her watch again.

I've really got to get going, she thought. *And I do have to have a conversation with Jane, or even Jeff; maybe there's something*

I can do to make this whole mess go away.

"Thanks," Emma said, pushing her chair away from the table. "I've got to get going."

"I guess we didn't help much, huh?" Carrie said.

"You tried," Emma said with a sigh.

"I'm telling you, Em, my advice was on the money—no pun intended," Sam said. "You need to find a way to out-connive your conniving mother."

"I think at the moment the best I can do is to find a good lawyer," Emma replied. She hugged Carrie, then Sam. "I love you guys. Thanks for trying."

"Let us know what happens with Kurt," Carrie reminded Emma.

"Sure," Emma said. But at that moment, Emma didn't feel very sure at all.

"So the thing is," Emma said, "can my mother get away with it?"

"Possibly, Emma," Jane said thoughtfully as she absent-mindedly tapped her pencil on the desk. "Quite possibly."

It was 8:20 that evening, and Emma and Jane were sitting together in Jane's home office. Jane had switched on her halogen lamp, and the office was bathed in bright light.

Emma had asked Jane right after dinner if she could talk to her privately about a personal problem, and Jane had immediately said yes. She'd ushered Emma into her home office, and, after Emma had made a few false starts, asked her to tell the story about Kurt and her mother from the very beginning.

Emma did, and it took her fifteen full minutes.

I feel weird coming to Jane, Emma thought. *I mean, she's my employer, not my attorney. But she was so helpful to me when I almost married Kurt—she even lent me her own bridal gown when I couldn't find one that I liked—that I know she'll be willing to help me now.*

"Have you thought about calling your father?" Jane queried.

"Yes," Emma answered slowly.

"Why don't you?" Jane pressed. "Perhaps he has more influence with your mother than you do. And I thought he liked Kurt."

"He does," Emma said. "But he's got his

141

own problems right now. How can I go to him with mine?"

"He might want to try to help you," Jane said gently. "Aren't your parents seeing each other again?"

Emma shrugged. "They were. But now that my father's lost so much money in the crash, my mother thinks he's kind of a fool."

"A lot of bright people lost money," Jane commented, still playing with the pencil. "*We* lost money."

"You did?" Emma asked, amazed. "I'm so sorry, I didn't even think to—"

"It's okay," Jane said quickly. "We didn't lose a lot. Nothing we couldn't afford not to have right away."

"So," Emma queried, steering the conversation back to her problem. "Can she do it? Can my mother just cut me off?"

Jane shifted in her chair. "For the will, the answer is yes. She can rewrite her will anytime she wants to."

"Great," Emma muttered.

"But I wouldn't worry about the will," Jane counseled. "Your mother is young and healthy—she's not planning to die anytime soon."

"Not unless I kill her," Emma said.

Jane smiled. "Somehow I doubt that you'll inherit her estate if you do."

"I'll try to keep that in mind," Emma said. "Although at the moment I'd call it justifiable homicide."

"Let's look at some practical matters," Jane said. "Who's the trustee on your trust?"

"I don't know," Emma said honestly. "I never bothered to ask."

Jane listened to Emma's answer, expressionless, but Emma could see that she was amazed that Emma knew so little about how her family money was managed.

And she had no idea of how rich I actually was—I can see that now, too! Emma thought. *Why do I feel embarrassed talking about all this with her? Why should I feel sheepish? My family didn't steal the money. They inherited it!*

"Well, I won't lie to you, Emma," Jane said, finally putting the pencil down. "The trust could be a problem."

"You mean to tell me that my mother can

have total say over everything I say and do? That if she doesn't like what I do she can just cut me off without a penny?" Emma asked incredulously.

"Maybe," Jane said. "It depends."

"Depends on what?"

"On how the trusts were set up, and whether your mother is executor, and whether the beneficiaries can be changed—things like that."

"*What?*" Emma asked, totally puzzled. She hadn't understood a word Jane had said.

Jane laughed. "That's why everyone hates lawyers. No one can understand us."

"Explain it to me simply," Emma suggested.

"The bottom line is," Jane said slowly, "that while in theory it's possible that your mother won't be able to get away with what she's planning, there's an even better chance that she can—that she'll be able to cut you off from the income on your trust funds until you're at least twenty-one years old."

"How am I supposed to respond to that?" Emma cried.

"I'm afraid, honey," Jane said, putting her hand over Emma's, "you're the only one who can answer that."

But I don't have an answer, Emma thought. She could feel tears coming to her eyes. *I have no idea what to do.*

"So, that's my lawyerly advice for tonight," Jane said, rising to her feet. "Anything else I can help you with?"

"Not really," Emma said sadly, staying in her seat.

Jane hesitated a moment, then sat back down. "Let me offer you one piece of unsolicited advice," she said.

"Anything," Emma said. "Because I am totally confused."

"Your life could be very unpleasant for the next year and a half," Jane said matter-of-factly, "until you turn twenty-one."

"Why?" Emma asked.

"Because your mother has invented a new weapon, a new atomic bomb," Jane explained. "If she thinks she can get you to do what she wants by threatening to use it, you're going to be seeing a lot of it."

"Meaning if she can use her trump card

to get me to do what she wants this time, she'll use it again," Emma said.

"Right," Jane agreed. "What's to stop her? What if she decides she doesn't like Carrie and Sam?"

"She'd never do that," Emma said quickly.

"Honey, I'm not saying she would," Jane said softly. "I'm just saying what if. She's in a very powerful position, if you allow her to be."

"But just until I'm twenty-one," Emma said.

"That's right," Jane agreed. "That's when the trust goes to you directly. The question is, Emma, is it worth it?"

TEN

I can't believe I'm finally going to talk to Kurt, especially since I feel like I've talked to everyone else, Emma thought, pulling down the sun visor to shield her eyes as she drove the Hewitts' van along Shore Road toward the main beach. *It seems like it's been forever. In a way, it has.*

And the worst part of it is that I haven't decided what I want to say to him!

It was late the next morning, and Emma was finally going to see Kurt and talk to him about her conversation with Kat. In fact, Emma had tried to get in touch with him the night before, but Kurt had ended up having to work overtime and wasn't expected back home until past midnight.

I had the joy of having his father tell me that when I telephoned him, Emma recalled ruefully. *My first conversation with him since the almost-wedding. When he asked who it was and I told him, he sounded like he was ready to bite my head off. If I'd been there, he probably would have.*

Emma sighed as she stopped at a red light. Jane had graciously given Emma an hour off before lunch—but she had to be home at noon in order to make lunch for little Katie.

Emma pulled the van into the already crowded main beach parking lot and found a spot very close to the boardwalk. She hopped out of the car, locked it, and set the alarm, then climbed the short wooden ramp leading up to the boardwalk.

She spotted Kurt immediately. He was wearing a faded pair of jeans and a Boston Patriots logo T-shirt, and was stretched out full-length on one of the benches, his eyes closed, sunglasses on, sneakers on the boardwalk under the bench, seemingly without a care in the world.

Emma walked over to him and kissed him gently on the lips. Kurt opened his eyes with a start, and then smiled when he saw who it was.

"Nice greeting," he said, grinning more widely. He took off his sunglasses and kissed her again. "Very nice."

"You're welcome," Emma said, trying desperately to match his happy mood, but instead just feeling sick to her stomach.

"Is this the part where the handsome prince turns into a bullfrog?" Kurt asked, sitting up on the bench and sliding over so that Emma could join him on it. "Because I'm getting hungry for some flies. Yum yum!"

"You're not allowed to call yourself a prince," Emma joshed.

"Only you are?" Kurt asked.

"That's right."

"Why's that?"

"Because I'm the Ice Princess," Emma said, feigning great nobility.

"Okay, Ice Princess," Kurt teased. The morning sun glinted off the blond highlights in his light brown hair. "What did the big bad queen have to say to you?"

Somehow Emma couldn't muster the courage to tell Kurt the truth right away. "Oh, her usual queenly things," she said, making a lame joke.

Kurt regarded her for a moment, then said quietly, "She put on quite a show for us the other night on the beach."

"True," Emma agreed glumly.

"Well, now at least you know what she's doing on the island," Kurt pointed out. "It's driving her nuts that we're together again, right?"

"Right."

"So did she draw and quarter me at lunch? Serve me up as the main course? What?" Kurt asked.

"You really want to know?" Emma asked.

"I really want to know," Kurt replied, reaching for Emma's hand and taking it in his.

"Well, she . . . she kind of threatened me, actually," Emma explained, her voice quavering.

"I won't let her get away with it," Kurt

said gallantly. "I'll send my two sisters over to beat her up."

"It wasn't that kind of a threat," Emma replied. She turned to gaze at Kurt. *I love him so much and I'm about to hurt him again,* she thought to herself. *But it's not my fault! I can't control what my mother does!*

"I still don't get you," Kurt said, puzzled.

Emma sighed deeply. "It was a money threat," she explained, finally relieved to get it off her chest.

"I *still* don't get you," Kurt replied. "She's not going to pay for college or something ridiculous like that?"

"Much worse," Emma said. "She said she'd basically cut me off completely."

Kurt looked stunned. "Wait . . . are you saying she'd, like, disinherit you if we're together?"

The story spilled out of her. She told him exactly what her mother had said during their lunch at the country club, and also about her conversation with Jane the night before.

Kurt shook his head. "I'm just about speechless."

"That's how I felt, too," Emma said.

"Well, it's unique, I'll say that. I've never had to deal with a thirty-million-dollar ultimatum before."

"It's more than that," Emma said dully.

"I can't even count beyond thirty million," Kurt quipped with a wan smile. "The whole thing would be funny if it weren't so pathetic."

"How can you say that?" Emma cried.

"I mean the fact that she thinks she'll be able to get away with it—that's hilarious," Kurt explained. "Obviously she doesn't know you very well—but then she never did."

Emma was silent for a moment. A feeling of guilt washed over her. *I'm not nearly as perfect as he thinks I am,* Emma thought. *Should I tell him I haven't really decided what to do, whether I should stand up to my mother and lose all my money, or give in and not see Kurt for a year and a half? If I tell him I'm not sure what to do, how will he feel about me—about us?*

"Sam says we should just lie to her," Emma related, deciding to postpone the hardest subject as long as possible.

"You went and talked to Sam about this?" Kurt said unbelievingly.

"And Carrie," Emma said, shrugging. "I couldn't reach you!"

"Last one to know," Kurt mumbled, practically to himself. "Well, I don't blame you. Yesterday must have been tough for you."

"Horrible," Emma replied, giving his hand a gentle squeeze.

"So Sam said to lie," Kurt repeated. "That sounds like Sam."

"She said that my mother isn't playing by the rules with us," Emma said, "so we don't have to play by the rules with her."

"Meaning?"

"Meaning I should just tell her I'm not seeing you," Emma said quickly.

"Tell her you're not seeing me? Like, sneak around behind her back?"

"Just until I turn twenty-one," Emma said quickly, hastening to add, "when I get my money."

Kurt smiled grimly. "So I was kind of right. You *are* ashamed of me—"

"How can you think that?" Emma cried.

"Okay, that wasn't fair," Kurt agreed. "But you know I won't sneak around to see you. I don't play that game, not for any amount of money."

"I know that," Emma said. "I was just telling you what Sam said! Besides, even if we wanted to do it, we'd get caught. My mother would hire private eyes."

"I hate this," Kurt said. "It's totally unfair. *Your mother* is totally unfair."

"Well, your father is just as unfair to me," Emma shot back.

"I don't think so," Kurt said. "You don't see him handing me any ultimatums, do you?"

"No," Emma admitted.

"Besides," Kurt continued, "he's made his point of view pretty clear to me, and you don't see me debating what I should do." He gave Emma a penetrating look. "Because that's what's going on, isn't it? You're really debating what you should do."

"Your father isn't talking about a family fortune!" Emma cried.

"No," Kurt said. "He's not. But what difference does that make?"

"It's just a year and a half!" Emma contended. "It makes all the difference! Do you know what our life would be like with millions of dollars in the bank?"

Kurt looked at her, a shocked expression on his face. "Our life," he said quietly.

"What?" Emma asked, bewildered.

"You just said 'our life,'" he whispered.

"I did?" Emma said.

"You did," Kurt confirmed. "You asked me if I knew what our life would be like with millions of dollars in the bank."

"I g-guess I did," Emma stammered.

Kurt looked out at the ocean. "I just don't get you, Emma. You don't want us to plan a future, but at the same time you *do* want us to plan a future."

"I know I haven't been clear," Emma admitted. "I . . . I guess I should say what I really mean."

"That would be a good idea," Kurt agreed.

Emma stared at her hands. "I love you. And I do want to think about a future with you. But . . . I don't want to make promises that we might not be able to keep!"

"Which leaves us with *kind of* a future," Kurt translated wryly.

"Is that so awful?" Emma asked. "I'm not ready to be engaged, but I'm ready to say I love you with all my heart. I still think we should both do what we're planning to do in the fall, but that doesn't mean I want our relationship to end, because I don't!"

Kurt nodded slowly. "I get it, believe it or not."

"Really?" Emma asked hopefully.

"I think so," Kurt said. "Before, we went too far too fast, right?"

"Right!" Emma agreed.

"So what you're saying is that the depth of your love hasn't changed—you just want to be on a more long-term game plan."

"That's right!" Emma cried. "And I don't want to have to define it, except to say that I'm one hundred percent committed to you, and I hope you are to me."

"I am, babe," Kurt said huskily. "Rich or poor, sane or insane—"

Tears of happiness came to Emma's eyes. "I think you mean sane or insane *mother*."

"Right," Kurt agreed. "I don't know how she lucked out enough to get such a terrific daughter." Kurt leaned over and gave Emma the sweetest kiss in the world.

In that moment, all of Emma's doubts vanished.

"Jane Hewitt was right," she said firmly.

"What?" Kurt asked.

"Jane told me last night that if I gave in to my mother on this, Kat would just hold the money over me like a weapon forever."

"That's probably true," Kurt agreed, lightly playing with Emma's hair.

"I can't let her do it, Kurt," Emma said passionately. "No matter what."

"Are you sure?" Kurt asked her.

"Yes," Emma answered.

"You'd risk being poor for me?" Kurt asked softly.

"Not just for you," Emma replied earnestly. "For myself. If I let her do this now, she can just keep doing it and doing it. How do I live with myself then?"

Kurt gazed at Emma with a look of true admiration on his face. "I love you, Emma Cresswell," he said softly.

"You'd better," Emma replied, edging closer to him. "After all this, you'd better."

Kurt looked off into the distance. "I have to admit something to you. Sometimes I've thought about what it would be like if we were married and you had your fortune—"

"I always told you it would become *ours*," Emma reminded him.

"And I always told you I'd never touch it," Kurt said, folding his arms. "But I have thought about what we could do with that money, together. The foundations we could start, the difference we could make in the lives of a lot of poor kids who deserve a chance . . ."

"If I stand up to my mother, that's a chance we might never have," Emma pointed out. "I mean, I just don't know enough about the details of my trust fund to have any idea of how much money there would be."

"I know," Kurt said. He shrugged. "That's life!" He shielded his eyes from the sun and gave her a penetrating look. "Do you know what our life would be like *without* millions of dollars in the bank?"

"I have no idea," Emma said truthfully.

"Normal," Kurt replied, a smile coming over his face. "Very, very normal."

And he took her in his arms.

"Hello!" Kat Cresswell answered the phone in her usual girlish tone.

"Mother?" Emma breathed into the phone.

"Well, hello, Emma," Kat said pleasantly. "I'm so glad you called me. I've had the loveliest day. I went out sailing on the *Popes Afloat*!"

It was later that afternoon. Emma had left Kurt on the boardwalk and had come home to make lunch for Katie. Now Katie was taking an afternoon nap, Wills was at his friend Stinky's, and Ethan was at Club Sunset Island, and Emma had finally mustered the courage to call her mother.

I made a decision, she kept saying to herself. *I made the right decision. Then why is it I have so many doubts?*

"Wonderful," Emma said tonelessly.

"The Popes are fine people," Kat replied. "*Our* kind of people."

Meaning old-money rich, Emma translated. "They are boring," she told her mother flatly. "People don't magically become interesting because they have money."

Kat laughed a short laugh. "Emma, you are just so sensitive. I didn't mean anything by that!" she said, her voice still gay and light. "The Popes are old family friends, remember?"

"Right, Mother," Emma replied.

"It was so thoughtful of you to call," Kat continued, a question in her voice.

"You asked me to," Emma said, sitting back on her bed.

"Oh, don't be ridiculous, Emma," Kat replied. "Now, I trust we've put that silly little episode on the beach behind us."

"That depends, Mother," Emma said into the phone, her voice quiet and controlled. "I have. Have you?"

"Of course, Emma," Kat answered. "I won't give it another minute's thought! I'm so glad you've made the right choice."

"In my opinion, Mother, yes, I have," Emma said directly.

"Why, whatever do you mean, dear?" Kat questioned.

"I can't do what you want me to," Emma said. She was grasping the phone so tightly that her knuckles were white. "I can't not see Kurt. And it's totally unfair of you to try to make me stop."

"That's your decision?"

"Yes," Emma answered, cold sweat breaking out all over her.

"You're going to continue to see this boy, and deliberately ruin your future?" Kat challenged.

"Yes, I am going to see him," Emma said. "And no, I don't think I'm ruining my future."

"You are being stupid, Emma," Kat snapped, "and I did not raise my daughter to be stupid."

"You think what I'm doing is stupid? That is a matter of opinion, Mother," Emma replied. "I don't happen to think that money is the be-all and end-all of life."

"My darling, that is because you have always had it," Kat said. "You have no concept of living any other way."

"Well, if you force me to, then I guess I'll find out," Emma said, trying to sound braver than she felt.

"Oh, try it," Kat sneered. "Try it! You'll see what it's like having no money! See what it's like to live on a babysitter's salary!"

"You have no right to dictate to me," Emma emphasized, speaking slowly and deliberately. "I don't tell you who your friends should be, and you shouldn't tell me who my friends should be!"

"I'm your mother—" Kat began.

"That's funny," Emma cut in. "You keep insisting that you're my best friend."

"Your attempts at cleverness are tiresome, Emma," Kat said. She sighed. "You are doing this to hurt me, and don't think I don't know it."

"Believe it or not, this isn't about you!" Emma said, trying to control her voice. "You are not the center of the universe!"

Kat sighed into the phone. "I find it amazing, Emma, that everything you accuse me of is exactly what you are."

"I am not!" Emma cried.

"Oh, yes," Kat insisted. "You think that everything revolves around you, that you can just do whatever you want, anytime you want."

"That's not me at all," Emma said, tears coming to her eyes. "You're deliberately twisting everything around!"

"Oh, Emma," Kat sighed.

Emma took a ragged breath. "Look, Mother, Kurt and I aren't getting married.

We aren't even engaged. In the fall I'll be back at college and he'll be at the Air Force Academy."

"Good," Kat commented. "That's a long way from Goucher College."

"So couldn't you just take a wait-and-see attitude?" Emma begged. "That's all I'm asking."

"I don't see why I should," Kat said. "I think that what you are doing will hurt you in the long run. You could just get in deeper and deeper with this boy, and then what will happen?"

Emma didn't reply.

"Oh, Emma," Kat cajoled, "please. You're going to be sorry if you don't change your mind. Please think about it some more!"

"My mind is made up," Emma answered, tears streaming down her face.

"Fine," Kat replied. "But remember, you can change it."

"I won't, Mother," Emma said emphatically. "This time, I just won't."

ELEVEN

"Emma, I just can't believe you're actually doing this," Carrie said as a rotund, elegantly dressed woman led the three girls to a cozy corner table at an upscale new French restaurant in Portland.

"I can," Sam said, slipping gracefully into her seat. "I was meant to live like this."

"I quite agree," the hostess said in a thick French accent. "I hope you have a lovely evening, *mesdemoiselles*. My name is Angelique, and you do my restaurant honor with your beauty. If there is anything I can do for you, you need only glance in my direction." With a graceful nod, Angelique walked away.

"Wow, she's so big she makes Erin look thin," Sam whispered. "I bet when she travels the airline makes her buy two seats!"

"You're terrible," Emma scolded.

"She also has on the longest false eyelashes I've ever seen in my life," Sam added, evidently fascinated by the woman.

"And she draws her eyebrows on with a black eyebrow pencil," Carrie noted.

"She's like something out of a Fellini movie," Emma said, and giggled.

"Who's Fellini?" Sam asked, checking out some guys at a nearby table.

"Sam," Emma sighed, "you are such a Philistine."

"I don't know what that means, either," Sam admitted. "Try speaking English, even if we are in a French restaurant."

"She means you're culture-free," Carrie teased, placing her napkin on her lap.

"*Au contraire*," Sam said regally. "I was probably born into a royal family and I'm extremely cultured. Now, bring on the French dancing boys!"

Emma just smiled. After her showdown with her mother, she'd spent the rest of the afternoon babysitting Katie Hewitt, but she'd bounced between being incredibly exhilarated by her own plucky performance and being incredibly depressed by the thought of the future.

And then the realization had hit her.

I may not have money in the future, but I sure have it for tonight, Emma had realized. *My mother couldn't do anything until tomorrow, I'm sure. Why don't I take Sam and Carrie out for an incredibly glamorous dinner at an incredibly glamorous restaurant? The three of us might never get the chance to do this again!*

So Emma, who had the evening off anyway, had asked Jane Hewitt for a recommendation. Jane suggested Les Marais, a new French restaurant that had opened the year before in Portland. The restaurant was housed in an elegant building that dated back to the early nineteenth century.

Emma didn't have much trouble convincing Sam and Carrie to join her, especially after she'd told them about her conversation with Kurt and her telephone call with her mother.

And now they were at Les Marais. They'd taken the ferry from the island over together, and the restaurant was located just a short walk from the Portland ferryport.

"You know, we are the three foxiest things in here," Sam said, leaning closer to her friends.

"Why do you always compare your looks to everyone else's?" Carrie said irritably.

"Everyone does that," Sam replied.

"I don't," Carrie said.

"Liar, liar, pants on fire," Sam sang. "You look at other girls to see if they have big hips because you think you have big hips. And I look at other girls to see if they have hooters because I don't have hooters. It's a girl thing."

"It's an insecurity thing," Carrie corrected.

"Whatever," Sam said breezily. "Anyway, tonight all three of us are seriously babe-aliscious!"

She's right, Emma thought, happy to be sitting there with her two best friends. *Even if our styles are completely different!*

Emma had on a simple, elegant sleeveless white silk shift with a white chiffon overlayer. Carrie had on a long floral-print dress that flowed out into a graceful A-line, and Sam had on one of her latest Sam-styles—a short piece of black velvet wrapped around her hips, sarong style, and clasped with a series of rhinestone hearts. On top she wore an antique bed jacket to which she had glued black velvet buttons, and she had a black velvet ribbon in her hair.

Sam sniffed the air. "We stink good, too," she said with a grin.

They were all wearing Sunset Magic perfume, the scent that Emma and Carrie had invented with the help of Erin Kane's father.

"Who knows, Emma?" Carrie said. "Maybe Sunset Magic will be such a huge success that you won't even miss the family money."

Emma sighed. So far they were only selling perfume in a few locations on the island, such as the Cheap Boutique. "We'll really have to expand if that's ever going to happen," she said.

"Every place that's selling it keeps reordering it," Carrie pointed out.

"*Mesdemoiselles*," a tuxedoed waiter said, handing each of them a heavy menu with a ruby suede cover. He was medium height, with thick black hair, dark eyes, and a gorgeous face. "My name is Jacques. I am your waiter this evening."

"Emma speaks perfect French, Jacques," Sam volunteered, nodding in the direction of her friend.

"*Ah bon?*" Jacques asked with delight. "*C'est vrai, vous parlez français?*"

"*Je peux m'exprimer un peu,*" Emma replied softly, in a perfect accent, modestly telling Jacques that she could express herself a little.

"From your accent," Jacques said, "it is obvious that you speak more than a little French."

"*Merci mille fois,*" Emma said. "A thousand thanks."

"But we speak English tonight for your friends, *d'accord?*"

"*D'accord,*" Emma said happily. "Okay." For some reason, she was feeling at the moment quite carefree, as if a weight had been lifted off her shoulders.

"You would care for some wine?" Jacques asked. Then, without waiting for the girls to answer, he added, "I'll send the *sommelier*."

"*Non, merci. De l'eau minerale, c'est tout,*" Emma replied.

"What was all that?" Sam asked.

"Ask your friend," Jacques said with a wink. He turned to head back to the front of the restaurant.

"He offered to send over the wine steward," Emma explained. "*Sommelier* is French for wine steward. But I told him that all we wanted was some mineral water."

"I knew that," Sam said with dignity. "I was just testing you." She eyed Jacques as he walked away. "How about if I order Jacques to go?"

All three girls looked at their menus.

They were entirely in French.

"I'm having the left side of the menu," Sam announced, putting her menu aside.

"All I studied was Spanish, so I'll let you order for me," Carrie said to Emma. "You know what I like."

"Sam?" Emma asked expectantly.

"Go ahead," Sam said, agreeing with Carrie. "But no snails, no rabbit, no baby cows, no baby sheep, no brains, no liver, no other internal organs, no raw anything, and nothing you can't buy in a supermarket in Kansas."

Emma smiled. "I promise I won't kill you," she said. And when their waiter came back, she ordered cassoulet, a kind of bean stew, for Sam, and grilled turbot, a fish that was often hard to find in American restaurants, for Carrie. For herself, she selected sautéed quail, a dish she'd had before and loved.

The service at Les Marais was impeccable. When the waiter had disappeared, two other servers arrived with warm mushroom salads, which they placed in front of the girls. And then they too disappeared.

"Who are they, Jacques's assistants?" Sam asked, picking up her fork. "Jacques-in-training?" She cautiously took a bite of her salad. "I could live like this."

"Me, too," Carrie echoed. "Only I'd gain about five pounds a week." She chewed on a mushroom and closed her eyes. "Mmm, this is so good."

"I wonder if I'll miss living like this," Emma said thoughtfully. "I don't think so."

Sam made the sound of a TV game-show buzzer. "Wrong answer."

"Why do you say that?" Emma asked, taking another bite of her salad.

"Because," Sam said matter-of-factly, "it's all you know. You've never had to earn your own money. Never ever ever."

"Come on, Sam," Emma defended herself. "I'm earning my own money this summer."

"That's true," Carrie chimed in.

"Please," Sam said, "let me ask you a question. Just how much money have the Hewitts paid you so far this summer?"

"What does that have to do with anything?" Emma replied.

"Everything," Sam said. "Do you know?"

"No," Emma admitted. "I know how much I make a week, though."

"I know to the penny how much Dan Jacobs has paid me," Sam said.

"Not enough," Carrie joked, nibbling on

a piece of Boston lettuce from her own salad.

"True," Sam said quickly. "But I know Carrie knows how much she's saved this summer. Right?"

Carrie nodded.

"And you don't, Emma, do you?" Sam asked.

Emma shook her head.

I honestly have no idea how much. I just endorse Jeff Hewitt's check and send it on to my financial manager in Boston, Emma thought, a little embarrassed.

"Emma Cresswell," Sam continued, "your world is about to get rocked."

"I can handle it," Emma said with dignity. "I'm not afraid to work."

"Let's assume your mom still pays for Goucher," Sam began.

"Oh, of course she will," Emma said. "It's her alma mater. She's more than thrilled that I'm going to college there, and she's relieved that it will keep me far away from Kurt."

"Okay, so she'll do the college thing," Sam said. "But you're still going to need something to live on."

Emma laughed. "Sam, my mother would never cut that off. It's the extras I won't have money for."

"How do you know?" Sam challenged.

"The scandal alone would kill her!" Emma exclaimed. "How would she explain to her friends if her daughter didn't have decent clothes or live in the right apartment? Believe me, that won't change."

"I don't know how you can be so certain," Carrie said, patting her mouth with her napkin.

"Please," Emma said a bit sharply, "I'm certain."

"Okay," Sam said, "but let's assume for a moment that dear Momma cuts off the money for that, too. Then what?"

Emma shook her head. "I'd be in real trouble," she admitted.

"What could you do to earn money?" Sam asked.

"I'd get a job!" Emma said defensively. "Lots of people work and go to college!"

Sam raised her eyebrows at Emma. "Do you know how much they make?"

"I don't know," Emma said crossly. "Not much, I suppose."

"I bet you don't even know what the minimum wage is!" Sam exclaimed.

She's right, Emma realized. *I have no idea.* "What is it?" she asked in a low voice.

"Not even five dollars an hour," Sam said with disgust.

"That's horrible!" Emma replied. "No one could live on that! Congress needs to pass a law!"

"Emma," Carrie said gently, "Congress *did* pass a law. That's who sets the minimum wage."

Emma slumped a little in her seat, embarrassed. And then question after question started to form in her mind.

What am I going to do about health insurance? Emma asked herself. *How am I going to live? Who can live on five dollars an hour? How can I pay the insurance on my car? Who's going to pay for my tickets home from school for the holidays? What kind of part-time job can I find? What experience do I have?*

She put her fork down with trembling fingers. "I seem to have lost my appetite," she said shakily.

"I didn't mean to bum you out," Sam

said. "But I don't know if you're being realistic about what you're heading for."

Oh my God, have I gone out of my mind? Emma thought. *I must have been crazy to say what I said to my mother!*

"Emma?" Carrie asked, a look of concern on her face. "Are you okay?"

Sam dipped her napkin into the glass of water and patted it on Emma's face. "You all right, girlfriend? You're so pale!"

Emma shook her head slightly. "I'm okay," she said quietly. "I think I just had a panic attack. Or the start of one."

Carrie took her hand. "It's scary, huh? What you did."

"Yes," Emma said simply. "I still think I did the right thing, but . . ." She didn't finish the rest of her statement. She wasn't even sure what it was she wanted to say.

"Well, I for one couldn't do what you're doing," Sam admitted. "No way José. The guy would keep for a year and a half, and then we'd both be rich and Mom could kiss my rich—"

"Assets?" Carrie quipped.

"Something like that," Sam agreed.

"I don't believe you," Emma said. "You

wouldn't give Pres up for a year and a half for any amount of money in the world."

"I might," Sam said.

Emma took a deep breath. "You guys," she said, looking at her friends, "this isn't going to be easy. It's just dawning on me how tough it's going to be."

"It's okay, Em," Carrie said.

"We're with you, girlfriend," Sam added.

"Thanks," Emma said gratefully. "Because I see now I'm going to need all the help I can get."

"L'addition, mademoiselle," Angelique said as she handed the check to Emma. Emma smiled and took it. "Dinner was satisfactory?"

"Magnifique," Sam said. "That means 'magnificent,' right?"

"Right," Emma agreed.

"The little French chocolates at the end were to die for, by the way."

The hostess bowed her head gracefully. "Our pleasure, *mademoiselle*."

"Tonight," Emma said, trying for a brave grin, "I can still pay for this. I don't know about tomorrow."

Her friends smiled sympathetically as Emma reached into her bag, took out one of her credit cards, and handed it to Angelique.

"Aren't you going to add it up?" Carrie asked.

"Oh, sure," Emma said sheepishly. She usually didn't even bother. She gave the bill a cursory glance. Dinner for the three of them was more than two hundred dollars, but it had been worth it.

What will two hundred dollars mean to me in the future? she thought anxiously. *How many meals will it buy? How many bills will it pay? And how can my own mother do this to me?*

Emma gave the credit card and the check back to Angelique.

"It's fine," she told her. "Please add eighteen percent as a gratuity."

"*Merci, mademoiselle, revenez-y,*" the hostess said, asking the girls to please return again sometime. Then she turned away to go handle the transaction.

Emma smiled at her friends. Not only had they shared an absolutely incredible meal, but Sam and Carrie had given her all kinds of really practical advice. *Not that I thought I'd ever need advice on how to take care of money*, Emma thought. *But now it seems like I have a lot to learn.*

A few moments later, Angelique returned.

"*Excusez-moi, mademoiselle, mais il y a un petit problème,*" she said to Emma. "*Pouvons-nous parler un peu, en privé?*"

"What's she saying?" Sam demanded.

"Excuse me a moment," Emma said. "She wants to talk to me."

"She probably wants you to come back tomorrow and do the whole thing over again, which would be cool with me as long as I'm invited," Sam quipped.

Emma got up from the table, and Angelique led her a discreet distance away.

"There is a small problem with your credit card," she said to Emma.

"A problem?" Emma echoed.

"Yes," Angelique replied. "It was turned down."

"There must be some error," Emma said confidently.

"Certainly," Angelique agreed diplomatically. "Do you have another?"

"Of course," Emma said.

180

"Then follow me, please." Angelique motioned to an alcove, and Emma followed her.

Angelique ran the new credit card through the approval machine.

Rejected, read the message.

They tried another.

Rejected.

"As you say, there must be some error," Angelique said coolly. "But surely you will settle the matter."

Emma's heart was pounding. *Oh, my God,* she thought. *She actually did it. My mother canceled all my credit cards. I can't believe it! Not even one left for emergencies.*

With shaking fingers Emma fished around in her purse. *I never keep that kind of cash in my purse,* Emma thought in a panic.

She came up with seven dollars, two quarters, and some lint.

"Perhaps *mademoiselle* would care to write a check," Angelique said. Her face was not looking nearly as friendly as it had a short while before.

Emma gulped hard. *I don't have a check-*

ing account, she thought. *I never bothered to start one.*

She knew Carrie had one, though, at the local bank. In it was the money Carrie was scrupulously saving up for the fall at Yale.

"Excuse me just a moment," Emma told Angelique.

Then she did one of the hardest things she'd ever had to do in her life. She walked over to Carrie and with the greatest of embarrassment asked Carrie to loan her the money to pay their bill.

TWELVE

I'm poor, Emma thought as she stared up at the ceiling in the half light of dawn. *I'm totally, completely poor.*

It was very early the next morning. Emma hadn't slept much. Instead she'd tossed and turned, replaying over and over again the awful moment from the night before when she'd had to ask Carrie to pay the dinner check.

"I'll pay you back," Emma had promised Carrie fervently as they walked out of the restaurant. Her face had been red with humiliation. "I promise."

"Em, it's not important," Carrie had

said. "You didn't know your mother had yanked your credit cards."

"That doesn't matter," Emma had replied. "I insisted we go out to that expensive restaurant and I'll take responsibility for the check."

On the ferry back to the island, Emma had closed her eyes and leaned against the railing, overcome with feelings of helplessness and hopelessness.

I remember the time Sam needed to borrow money from me for her friend Marina, who got stranded overseas, Emma recalled. *And I remember how they said they'd pay me back every penny, and they eventually did. I never, ever thought the shoe would be on the other foot. I had no idea how they felt, but now I do. Embarrassed. Humiliated.*

As soon as Emma had gotten back to the Hewitts', she'd tried to call Kat at the Sunset Inn, only to find she'd already checked out. *And she didn't even tell me,* Emma thought bitterly, *any more than she bothered to tell me she was cutting off my credit cards right away. How could my own mother treat me this way?*

After tossing and turning for another hour or so, Emma finally gave up on trying to sleep. She pulled on some leggings and a sweatshirt, and padded downstairs to make herself some tea. To her surprise, she found Jane sitting in the kitchen, staring dreamily out at the sunrise.

"Hi," Emma said quietly.

"Oh, you startled me," Jane said. "What are you doing up so early?"

"So late, you mean," Emma said, going for the tea kettle. "I haven't really slept at all."

"Still trying to decide what to tell your mom?" Jane asked, sipping her coffee.

"Oh, that's done," Emma said, feeling exhausted. She turned the heat on under the tea kettle. "I stood up to her ultimatum, all right, and do you know what she did? She immediately cut off all my credit cards without telling me. Last night at the restaurant every single one of my credit cards was refused. I had to get Carrie to pay for dinner. It was the most humiliating moment of my life."

"Wow, she really did pull a power play, huh?" Jane sympathized.

"I just can't believe it!" Emma cried. "Even as it's happening to me, it doesn't seem real!"

"Your life is about to change," Jane said. "A lot."

"I can see that," Emma agreed bitterly. "And why? Because I want to choose my own boyfriend? Because I want to run my own life?"

The kettle began to whistle and Emma poured the water into her cup, dropping in a bag of herbal tea. "I'm sorry, Jane," she murmured. "I shouldn't be taking this out on you." She turned around and leaned against the counter. "What are you doing up so early, anyway?"

"Thinking," Jane said with a secret smile.

"At dawn?" Emma asked.

Jane nodded. "Please don't say anything to the kids, but . . . I think I'm pregnant."

"You're *what*?" Emma asked.

"Pregnant," Jane repeated. "You know. Knocked up. With child. In the family way."

"I'm sorry," Emma said, flustered. "I'm just . . . surprised, I guess."

"Me, too," Jane said with a laugh. "We didn't exactly plan it. But I'm happy as well."

Emma took the teabag out of her cup and brought her tea over to the table. "But aren't you . . . kind of old?" Emma asked delicately.

"Emma, I'm not even forty yet," Jane said, an amused look on her face. "Married people my age really do have sex and get pregnant, you know."

"Oh, I'm sorry, Jane, I'm acting like an idiot!" Emma cried. She got up and hugged her employer. "I'm very happy for you!"

"Thanks," Jane said, returning the embrace. "It's not for sure yet, though. I haven't taken a pregnancy test. But I've been having all the symptoms." Jane took a sip of her coffee. "Decaf," she said with a smile, holding up her mug. She put it down again.

"I had kind of a rough time with Katie, and I was a lot younger then," Jane continued. "If I am pregnant, I'm going to need to rely on you more this summer."

"Of course!" Emma readily agreed. "I'll help any way I can!"

And then the wheels in Emma's head started to turn. *I'll have to do more work for the same money,* she realized. *I never had to give any thought to that kind of thing before. But now every penny will count. I know what Sam would do. She'd ask for a raise. That's what I should do.*

"Jane . . ." Emma began hesitantly.

"Yes?"

"I was wondering," Emma said. "Uh, now that I'll have to live on my salary from this job . . ."

"Yes?"

Oh, God, I hate this! It's so tacky and demeaning! Emma thought miserably. She took a deep breath. "Well, I was wondering if you might consider giving me a raise."

Jane looked at Emma thoughtfully. "We agreed on a certain wage for this summer," she said.

"Yes," Emma acknowledged. "But my circumstances were different."

"That's true," Jane mused. "However, we are paying you the going rate for an au pair on the island, you know."

"I know," Emma said miserably, feeling lower than she'd ever felt. "But . . . I need the money."

"I'll discuss it with Jeff," Jane said. "Okay?"

"Okay," Emma agreed. "You know I would never quit or anything, Jane," she added quickly. *Now I actually need this job,* Emma realized. *It feels completely different from always being in the driver's seat, knowing that no matter what happened I never had to worry about money, ever.*

Now I'm poor. Poor. Poor.

I'll have to live on a budget. I'll have to find out how much my expenses are and if I can live on my salary. I have to—

"Emma, I don't mean to interfere," Jane said, interrupting Emma's train of thought, "but I really do suggest you think about calling your dad."

"He's more broke than I am," Emma said sadly.

"Honey, when a rich person declares bankruptcy, that doesn't mean they're penniless," Jane said gently. "There are ways to avoid losing every cent, and I'm sure your father knows what they are."

"There are?"

Jane smiled kindly. "You really don't know anything about money at all, do you?"

"I don't suppose I do," Emma admitted. She felt a tightening in her throat; tears threatened to spill from her eyes.

Jane put her hand over Emma's. "It's going to be okay, Emma. I know all this is a shock for you. But your mother might change her mind. Or your father might be able to intervene with her, or help you himself. And even if neither of those things happens, you're young, healthy, and intelligent. You'll learn to cope without money."

"Like the rest of the world, you mean," Emma said.

"Well, yes, actually," Jane agreed. "Like *most* of the rest of the world. I'm not telling you it's going to be easy, or that it isn't hard to be poor when all you've ever been is rich, but I have a lot of faith in you."

"You do?" Emma whispered, gulping hard.

"I do," Jane said firmly. "You are an amazing person. You're going to be fine."

"Thanks," Emma said shakily. She pushed

back her chair. "I think I *will* go call my dad," she said, getting up. "But I just hate to burden him with this."

"Honey, give him a chance to be a dad to you," Jane advised. "Let him be there for you."

"Okay, I will," Emma agreed. Impetuously she leaned over and kissed Jane's cheek. "You're the greatest, Jane. Thank you. And I'm so happy for you, about the baby."

"It's not for sure yet!" Jane called to Emma as she ran up the stairs to call her dad.

Emma quickly dialed her father's number in Boston, then paced while the phone rang. *Please be there,* she chanted in her mind. *I really need you to be there.*

"Brent Cresswell," her father's voice barked into the phone.

"Daddy!" Emma exclaimed with relief.

"Emma, sweetheart! This is a surprise! It's only seven-thirty in the morning!"

"I know," Emma said, sitting on her bed. Nervously she wrapped the phone cord around her fingers. "But I really need to talk to you. Has Mother said anything to you about her visit to Sunset Island to see me?"

"Hardly," Brent said dryly. "She won't even return my phone calls."

"You mean she won't talk to you just because you lost money in the stock market?" Emma exclaimed.

"So it seems," Brent confirmed.

"But that's absurd!"

"Oh, it's just one of Kat's games," Mr. Cresswell said. "She'll deign to speak to me eventually. Remember, I've known your mother a long time. So she came to visit you, did she?"

"No, she came to blackmail me," Emma said bitterly. Then she quickly explained to her father exactly what had happened.

For a long moment there was silence on the other end of the phone.

"I . . . I don't know what to say, Emma," her father finally managed. "I can't believe your mother would do something so cruel."

"I can," Emma said. "She did it."

"I'll go over there this afternoon and talk with her," Brent promised.

"Would you, Daddy?" Emma asked hopefully.

"Yes, of course I will. But . . . I don't know if it will do any good."

"It has to!" Emma cried. *If Daddy can't get Mother to change her mind, what will I do?* she thought, scared. *Maybe . . . maybe he could give me money now and then, just so I can make ends meet. But . . . he hasn't offered. Maybe Jane was wrong, and he really has nothing left!* She told herself that she should just ask him, but the memory of how humiliated she had felt when she'd asked Carrie for a loan came rushing back to her, and she just couldn't do it.

Mr. Cresswell sighed into the phone, breaking into her thoughts. "It's her family's money, sweetheart. I came into our marriage as poor as a church mouse, as the saying goes. I couldn't believe that a rich, beautiful woman like that would marry a bum like me. No one else could, either."

"You weren't a bum!" Emma insisted.

"Well, I certainly was poor, which meant I was a bum in the eyes of her family and her crowd," Brent explained. "And now . . .

well, I suppose now that I'm broke, I'm a bum again."

Emma felt as if a hand were squeezing her heart. *I hate the self-pity in his voice,* she thought. *I want him to be strong and brave. I want him to be able to make everything okay for me!*

But even as she said good-bye to her father, she had the terrible, sinking feeling that he wasn't going to be able to make everything all right.

"We're leaving!" Jane called upstairs. "We'll be back around seven or so, okay?"

"Okay," Emma called down.

It was a few hours later, and Jane and Jeff were taking Katie into their Portland office with them. Emma had tried to keep extra busy all morning, making up lavish games for Katie to play so that she could keep her mind off her own trouble. It hadn't worked. She felt as if she was dragging a dead weight of anxiety and depression around with her.

"Emma, why can't you come, too?" Katie asked, running into Emma's room and jump-

194

ing into her lap. "The office is fun. We can use the fax machine!"

"I think I'll stay here and make you all a wonderful dinner for when you get home. Okay, sweetie?" Emma kissed the little girl on the top of her head.

"Okay," Katie agreed.

"Katie, honey, let's go!" Jeff called.

"Coming!" Katie waved to Emma and ran downstairs. Emma heard the front door shut, and she threw herself down on her bed.

Peace and quiet, which I can't even appreciate, she thought glumly. *Maybe I should use this time to make a budget.* She sat up and reached for her journal, which she kept in the drawer of her nightstand.

I remember when my aunt Liz gave this to me, she thought, fondly running her hand over the tapestry cover. *It was when I first came to the island. I was so scared and hopeful. I wanted so much to fit in, and not have everyone know how rich I was. I wanted to be just like everyone else. Funny—I just got my wish, in a bizarre sort of way.*

Emma sat up quickly. *Aunt Liz! Why*

didn't I think of Aunt Liz! She's as crazy about me as I am about her! She won't let Mother pull this!

Quickly Emma dialed her aunt's number in New York City. The phone rang and rang, and then the answering machine picked up. "Hi, this is Liz. I'm in Sweden at the International Greenpeace Conference through the end of this month, though I will call in periodically for messages. Feel free to leave me one at the beep."

"Aunt Liz, it's Emma. Please call me when you get this message. Thanks." She hung up the phone, feeling sad and hopeless.

What makes me think Aunt Liz can get Mother to change her mind, anyway? Emma realized. *Kat never listens to Liz. She thinks she's a renegade.*

The phone rang, startling Emma. She picked it up quickly.

"Hewitt residence, Emma Cresswell speaking," she said automatically.

"The beautiful Emma? The one with the softest lips on Sunset Island?" Kurt's voice said through the phone.

"If you say so," Emma agreed, unable to come up with a witty reply.

"Hey, babe, what's wrong?" Kurt asked. "Are you okay?"

"I'm all right," Emma assured him. "I'm just a little . . . sad about this situation with my mother."

"That's why I called," Kurt said. "I was thinking how incredible you are, standing up to your mother this way. I wanted to tell you that."

"Thanks," Emma said listlessly.

"I've really been giving it a lot of thought," Kurt continued. "I mean, my dad, your mom, they just don't understand. And we can't let either of them run our lives, right?"

"Right," Emma agreed.

"I know this whole thing is a big shock for you," Kurt continued. "But it's going to be fine. I'm with you every step of the way."

But you're used to being poor, Emma wanted to say. *I'm not!* She didn't say that, though.

"Listen, are you sure you're okay?" Kurt asked again, his voice concerned. "Do you want me to come over there? I've got the cab, but I could stop by and—"

"No, no, I'm okay, really," Emma assured him, even though she didn't feel okay at all.

"Can I see you tonight?" Kurt asked softly. "How about a late-night picnic under the stars? I get rid of the hack about ten."

"That sounds wonderful," Emma said, and it really did, but she couldn't shake her feeling of sadness and worry.

"Great," Kurt said. "Em, I just want you to know, I really admire you."

"You do?" she said dubiously.

"I do," Kurt said. "It's not every person who would be able to do what you're doing. You really have character, babe. You are one amazing girl."

"Thanks," Emma said softly.

"I believe that when I see you I can show you just how amazing I think you are," Kurt added huskily.

"It's a deal," Emma agreed, and said good-bye.

Emma lay back down on her bed, and tears formed in the corners of her eyes.

Snap out of it, she told herself. *Your life isn't over; it's just changing. You can handle this.*

"Anybody home?" a voice called from downstairs.

Emma recognized Carrie's voice, and she walked into the hallway. Carrie and Sam were looking up at her.

"Oh, good, you're here," Carrie said.

"We were on our way to the Play Café for lunch and we decided to stop and kidnap you," Sam said. "Do you have to work?"

"No," Emma said, coming down the stairs. "Jane and Jeff took Katie to Portland, Wills is at Stinky's, and Ethan is at the day camp."

"Cool," Sam said happily. "Let's go pig out!"

Reprieve! Emma thought happily. *Being with Carrie and Sam will cheer me up. And I always love to go to the Play Café, so—*

And then she realized that she didn't have enough money to go to the Play Café for lunch. She had sent her last paycheck to the financial manager in Boston, and she had no idea what he did with it. She wasn't due to be paid again until the end of the following week. Which meant she couldn't afford to do anything.

"Thanks, anyway," Emma said. "I don't think so."

Carrie put her hand on Emma's arm. "Look, if this is about what happened at the restaurant last night—"

"It's not," Emma said quickly. "And remember, I'm paying you back every penny. Plus interest."

Carrie groaned. "Forget the interest, please."

"So why don't you want to go with us?" Sam asked, leaning against the wall. "Something I said? Something I did?"

"No, no, nothing like that," Emma assured her. "I'm just . . . uh . . . not hungry."

"Since when do you have to be hungry to go to the Play Café?" Sam questioned. "We're talking fine guy-watching, junk food, great music, and no kids to take care of. Who cares about hunger?"

"I need to . . . make dinner for the Hewitts," Emma said, trying to sound casual.

"What're you making that takes all afternoon?" Sam asked dubiously.

"It's a new recipe," Emma invented. "It's very complicated."

"Girlfriend," Sam said, "I may be dumb but I am not stupid. Now what is up with you?"

Emma sighed and plopped down on the bottom step. *These are my best friends and I can tell them the truth,* she thought. "I can't afford it," she said in a low voice.

"You can't—" Sam began.

"I'll treat," Carrie said quickly.

"No, no, I don't want you to treat!" Emma cried. "God, I hate this! This is so horrible!" She buried her face in her hands.

Without a word, Carrie and Sam took seats on either side of Emma.

"Arghhh, I can't stand this!" Emma exclaimed. "I can't believe Kat did this to me!"

"We know it's tough," Carrie said sympathetically.

"Yeah," Sam agreed. "It's one thing never to have had money, but it's another thing to have always had it and then lose it. Ouch."

"Sam and I were talking about it on the way over here," Carrie continued. "We both really admire you, Emma. Standing up to your mother the way you did, risking your inheritance . . ."

"It's mind-blowing!" Sam put in. "I mean, I always knew you were walking cool, but now I know you're at the head of the parade!"

Emma couldn't help it—tears sprang to her eyes. "No, no, I'm not!" she cried. "I'm a total fraud! Everyone keeps saying how wonderful I am, and how much integrity I have—Jane, and Kurt, and now you two—but I don't! I'm so scared I can't eat or sleep or even think! I'm not brave at all! I'm scared to death, and I feel as if this is the worst day of my life!

"Half the time I want to strangle my mother, just rip into her and tell her where to go, never even see her again. And half the time I picture myself driving to Boston and throwing myself on her mercy. I'd tell her she wins, and even though I love Kurt with all my heart, it's not such a big deal if I don't get to be with him for a year and a half, but it's a really big deal to be poor!"

She buried her face in her hands again. "You two must hate me. *I* hate me!"

There was silence for a long time. Emma finally lifted her tear-stained face and Carrie handed her a tissue from her purse.

"Thanks," Emma said nasally, blowing her nose. "God, I'm a wreck."

"Okay, I have to say it," Sam said. "My mind is totally blown. Do you know what this means? You, Emma Cresswell, are human! You are not an ice princess after all! Prick her, ladies and gentlemen of the jury, and she bleeds just like everyone else!"

"You are certifiable," Emma said, laughing through her tears. She blew her nose again.

"I think that what Sam is saying, in her own inimitable fashion," Carrie said, "is that we don't expect you to be brave and noble about this."

"Well, you should," Emma replied. "What right do I have to complain? Poor little rich girl who lost her inheritance. Big deal."

"In some ways yes, and in some ways no," Carrie said in her usual honest and practical fashion. She jiggled the car keys in her hand. "It definitely is a big deal. And I can understand how it would be scary."

"I don't know how to be poor," Emma said quietly.

"So you'll learn," Sam said. "Meanwhile, we still think you're the coolest."

"I'm not."

"Why, because you're scared and you have doubts?" Sam asked. "That's a perpetual state for me!"

Emma laughed and wiped away the last of her tears. "I have a lot to learn, you know that?"

"Don't we all," Carrie said. "Look, Kat may change her mind. She might just be trying to scare you into doing what she wants you to do. But even if it's forever, I know you, Emma, and you can handle it."

"I wish I thought as much of me as you think of me," Emma managed in a small voice as she twisted the tissue in her hands.

"You're, like, this totally amazing person," Sam told her. "You and Carrie can probably make your own fortune on Sunset Magic perfume, if you really decide to go for it. And if it's not that, it'll be something else. I know it will."

"Me, too," Carrie agreed.

"I wish I felt half as confident as you two," Emma whispered, gulping hard.

"Emma-bo-bemma," Sam said, "you have picked me up so many times! And some of those were times when I was so far down that it looked like up to me. And frankly, I never thought I had all that much to offer you, except for the fact that I am your basic laugh a minute." Sam smiled at Emma, and a rare shy look came over her face. "So if I can help you, I mean *really* help you, you'll really be giving *me* a gift, and that's the truth."

"One for all and all for one, remember?" Carrie told her. "You don't have to be perfect, Emma. You never did."

"Thanks," Emma said, tears leaking out of her eyes again. "I don't know what I'd do without the two of you."

"Fortunately that is something you never will have to know," Sam said, jumping up. "Now let's get our butts into the car and go chow down at the Play Café."

"But I—" Emma began.

"I, Samantha Bridges, will pay, thank you very much," Sam said grandly. "I refuse to take no for an answer. I've never had the chance to treat you before in my life, and I'm not about to miss out on my big opportunity."

"Thanks," Emma said, standing up. Carrie stood up, too. "I'm going to learn to do a budget and all that," Emma told her friends. "I promise."

"We know you will," Carrie said. "And we'll help you."

"No matter what," Sam said, "I still get to hate you now and then."

"Oh, and why is that?" Emma asked, grinning at her friend.

"Because you are the only girl I know who still looks gorgeous even when she's crying," Sam said, shaking her head. "There is truly no justice in the world."

"None," Carrie agreed.

"None at all," Emma seconded.

The three of them walked out the front door and the sunshine hit their faces.

"See, it's a beautiful day after all," Carrie told Emma softly.

"Absolutely awesome," Sam agreed. "You'd better believe it!"

Emma looked up at the blue sky, then at the smiling faces of her two best friends, and then, just a little, she began to believe it, too.

SUNSET ISLAND MAILBOX

Dear Sunset Sisters,

Hurray, we're back in action! Another summer of great Sunset Island books is coming your way, and I promise you're going to love it. Sunset Love was a lot of fun to write, and Sunset Fling, Sunset Tears, and Sunset Spirit are going to be just as much fun for you to read.

There's going to be excitement, lots and lots of romance . . . and some sad moments, too, because—as you always tell me in your letters—Sunset Island is very much like a real place.

A lot has been going on since my last letter to you in Sunset Passion. One cool thing is that the Cherie Bennett Believers Fan Club is now in full swing: If you write to me I'll send you information about it. Fan club members get all kinds of great stuff, including a list of "Sunset Sister penpals" from all over the world!

Another cool thing is that I had a bat mitzvah, which is a Jewish religious ceremony in which a person becomes an adult in the eyes of the community. Girls usually go through this when they turn thirteen, and (I know you will find this hard to believe) I am a little older than thirteen. Becoming a bat mitzvah took a year of study and preparation—I had to learn how to read

Hebrew, for example! All of it was totally worth it. Afterward, I had a huge party, and was joined by ten Sunset Island sisters from around the country!

So, Jeff and I have had a great few months—we've met a lot of you here in Nashville and on our various travels, and I've answered tons of letters from you. You know the drill: Every letter I get is personally read and personally answered. If you don't believe me, ask a friend who has written to me.

I'm looking forward to hearing from you soon, because I want this series to be everything you want it to be. Write and tell me what you're thinking!

See you on the island!
Best—
Cherie Bennett

Cherie Bennett
c/o General Licensing Company
24 West 25th Street
New York, New York 10010

All letters printed become property of the publisher.

Dear Cherie,

Hi! Jessene here—your loyal reader 4-ever. Okay, now the praise 'bout your books—blah, blah, blah, etc., etc., etc. Talk about Rollerblading, it's the latest craze here in Singapore. Have you tried it? It's very fun!

*Love,
Jessene Lim
Singapore*

Dear Jessene,

I love my readers in Singapore, way off in southeast Asia! I receive a lot of fan mail from there. No, I can't say I've ever tried Rollerblading. I used to be pretty good at roller skating, though. But I've got to admit that I'm really out of practice now!

Best,
Cherie

Dear Cherie,

I listened to your suggestions in my last letter on how to name characters in stories I write. Your suggestions helped me get an A- on a Language Arts final paper. Thanks very much. Are there going to be any more books for Darcy Laken?

*Your #1 Fan,
Cori Kabat
Park Ridge, IL*

Dear Cori,

Glad that I could be of help! Many readers write to ask me for tips about writing, and I try to give everyone at least one good idea. One way to name characters is to find a name that's memorable and reflects a character's personality . . . like Emma's, for example. You'll be glad to know that Darcy Laken will be making a lot of appearances on the island this summer!

Best,
Cherie

Dear Cherie,
I wanted to tell you how much I appreciated your taking me out to eat. I never thought I would ever get to meet you. Thanks for making my dreams come true. I enjoyed talking with you and Jeff very much. I will never forget what you did for me. It meant a lot!
Thanks so much,
Bobbi Bacon
Long Prairie, MN

Dear Bobbi,
It was a pleasure. We had an absolutely great time, too. And if other readers need actual proof that if they come to Nashville, and my schedule permits it, I'll take them out to lunch, your letter is it! When I say I really, truly care about my readers, it's not just talk.

Best,
Cherie

Read how Carrie, Emma, and Sam began their Sunset Island escapades. *Love. Laughter. Romance.* Dreams come true, and friendships last a lifetime.

SUNSET ISLAND™
CHERIE BENNETT

__SUNSET WEDDING	0-425-13982-4/$3.99
__SUNSET GLITTER	0-425-14101-2/$3.99
__SUNSET STRANGER	0-425-14129-2/$3.99
__SUNSET HEART	0-425-14183-7/$3.99
__SUNSET REVENGE	0-425-14228-0/$3.99
__SUNSET SENSATION	0-425-14253-1/$3.99
__SUNSET MAGIC	0-425-14290-6/$3.99
__SUNSET ILLUSIONS	0-425-14336-8/$3.99
__SUNSET FIRE	0-425-14360-0/$3.99
__SUNSET FANTASY	0-425-14458-5/$3.99
__SUNSET PASSION	0-425-14397-X/$3.99
__SUNSET LOVE	0-425-15025-9/$3.99
__SUNSET FLING (July)	0-425-15026-7/$3.99

Payable in U.S. funds. No cash orders accepted. Postage & handling: $1.75 for one book, 75¢ for each additional. Maximum postage $5.50. Prices, postage and handling charges may change without notice. Visa, Amex, MasterCard call 1-800-788-6262, ext. 1, refer to ad # 366

Or, check above books Bill my: ☐ Visa ☐ MasterCard ☐ Amex
and send this order form to: (expires)
The Berkley Publishing Group   Card#_____
390 Murray Hill Pkwy., Dept. B   ($15 minimum)
East Rutherford, NJ 07073   Signature_____
Please allow 6 weeks for delivery.   Or enclosed is my: ☐ check   ☐ money order

Name_____   Book Total $_____
Address_____   Postage & Handling $_____
City_____   Applicable Sales Tax $_____
                                 (NY, NJ, PA, CA, GST Can.)
State/ZIP_____   Total Amount Due $_____

CHERIE BENNETT BELIEVERS
FAN CLUB

Hey, Readers! You asked for it, you've got it!

Join your Sunset sisters from all over the world in the greatest fan club in the world...
Cherie Bennett Believers Fan Club!

Here's what you'll get:

★ a personally-autographed-to-you 8x10 glossy photograph of your favorite writer (I hope!).
★ a bio that answers all those <u>weird questions</u> you always wanted to know, like how Jeff and I met!
★ a three-times yearly newsletter, telling you <u>everything</u> that's going on in the worlds of your fave books, and me!
★ a personally-autographed-by-me membership card.
★ an awesome bumper sticker; a locker magnet or mini-notepad.
★ "Sunset Sister" pen pal information that can hook you up with readers all over the world! Guys, too!
★ and much, much more!

So I say to you – don't delay! Fill out the request form here, clip it, and send it to the address below, and you'll be rushed fan club information and an enrollment form!

Yes! I'm a Cherie Bennett Believer! Cherie, send me information and an enrollment form so I can join the **CHERIE BENNETT BELIEVERS FAN CLUB!**

My Name _____

Address _____

Town _____

State/Province _____ Zip _____

Country _____

CHERIE BENNETT BELIEVERS FAN CLUB
P.O. Box 150326
Nashville, Tennessee 37215 USA

items offered may be changed without notice

Nicholas Pine's
TERROR ACADEMY

Welcome to Central Academy.
It's like any other high school on the outside.
But inside, terror is in a class by itself.

__LIGHTS OUT	0-425-13709-0/$3.50
__STALKER	0-425-13814-3/$3.50
__SIXTEEN CANDLES	0-425-13841-0/$3.50
__SPRING BREAK	0-425-13969-7/$3.50
__THE NEW KID	0-425-13970-0/$3.99
__STUDENT BODY	0-425-13983-2/$3.99
__NIGHT SCHOOL	0-425-14151-9/$3.50
__SCIENCE PROJECT	0-425-14152-7/$3.50
__THE PROM	0-425-14153-5/$3.99
__THE IN CROWD	0-425-14307-4/$3.50
__SUMMER SCHOOL	0-425-14338-4/$3.50
__BREAKING UP	0-425-14398-8/$3.50
__THE SUBSTITUTE	0-425-14534-4/$3.99
__SCHOOL SPIRIT	0-425-14644-8/$3.99
__BOY CRAZY	0-425-14727-4/$3.99

Payable in U.S. funds. No cash orders accepted. Postage & handling: $1.75 for one book, 75¢ for each additional. Maximum postage $5.50. Prices, postage and handling charges may change without notice. Visa, Amex, MasterCard call 1-800-788-6262, ext. 1, refer to ad # 453

Or, check above books Bill my: ☐ Visa ☐ MasterCard ☐ Amex	
and send this order form to:	(expires)
The Berkley Publishing Group Card#_____	
390 Murray Hill Pkwy., Dept. B	($15 minimum)
East Rutherford, NJ 07073 Signature_____	
Please allow 6 weeks for delivery. Or enclosed is my: ☐ check ☐ money order	
Name_____	Book Total $_____
Address_____	Postage & Handling $_____
City_____	Applicable Sales Tax $_____
State/ZIP_____	(NY, NJ, PA, CA, GST Can.) Total Amount Due $_____